'What's going on?' she asked.

He took her hand and led her into the dining room, where the table was set for the meal, and beside her place were the roses. She walked across slowly and picked them up without speaking, then began to read the card that was with them.

'The flowers are beautiful.' She smiled. 'I'll go and get a vase.' Without further comment she left him standing there, while she went to the pantry where her mother kept such things on the top shelf.

He watched in silence as she arranged the flowers, and, with weddings very much on the agenda, he had a vision of her walking towards him down the aisle of the village church, in a dress of rustling ivory brocade and carrying cream roses.

In that moment he knew that was what he wanted. Kate in his life for ever.

Abigail Gordon loves to write about the fascinating combination of medicine and romance from her home in a Cheshire village. She is active in local affairs, and is even called upon to write the script for the annual village pantomime! Her eldest son is a hospital manager, and helps with all her medical research. As part of a close-knit family, she treasures having two of her sons living close by, and the third one not too far away. This also gives her the added pleasure of being able to watch her delightful grandchildren growing up.

Recent titles by the same author:

COUNTRY DOCTOR, SPRING BRIDE

BY
ABIGAIL GORDON

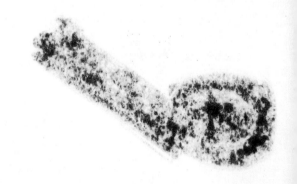

MILLS & BOON®
Pure reading pleasure

First published in Great Britain 2008
Harlequin Mills & Boon Limited,
Eton House, 18-24 Paradise Road, Richmond, Surrey TW9 1SR

© Abigail Gordon 2008

ISBN: 978 0 263 19892 8

Set in Times Roman 10½ on 12 pt
15-0408-49944

Printed and bound in Great Britain
by Antony Rowe Ltd, Chippenham, Wiltshire

COUNTRY DOCTOR, SPRING BRIDE

For my friend Elizabeth McInery

CHAPTER ONE

THE longing to be back with someone who loved her was so strong that Kate Barrington could almost taste it as she drove through the last few miles of the countryside where she'd been brought up.

She wanted to feel her mother's arms around her. To be back in her bedroom beneath the eaves of Jasmine Cottage so that she could weep away the anger and feeling of betrayal that had been with her over the past few days.

She was feeling as low as she'd ever felt in her life. Mentally because the wedding that she'd been dreaming of was not to be, along with the relationship that went with it, and physically because she felt ill.

It had come upon her the night before. Aching limbs, high temperature and vomiting, which had made her even more anxious to leave the southern counties where she'd been based for the last two years. There was nothing to keep her there any more. The job had folded at the same time as the wedding plans.

As she pulled onto the drive of the old stone house, loosely described as a cottage, with its four large bedrooms and spacious downstairs accommodation, Kate's mood was lifting. Here she was hoping to shut out some of the unhappiness that had erupted into her life. Any second the door would be flung open. Her mother would be there with arms outstretched and nothing would seem quite so bad.

She'd left a message on the answering-machine the night before to say she was coming home, and thought if there wasn't a fatted calf to greet her there would at least be some of the good home-cooked food that she'd missed so much while she'd been working away.

As she began to heave her cases out of the boot she saw that the door remained closed and the house had an empty look about it. Her heart sank. Where was her mother? she thought fretfully as her head throbbed and she shivered in the afternoon of a chilly autumn day.

If her mother had received her message she wouldn't have budged an inch. She had been begging her to come home ever since she'd split up with Craig. But there'd been as much to do in cancelling a wedding as there'd been in organising one, and she'd only just finished tidying up all the loose ends.

The house felt cold when she went inside and Kate wondered if it was because the heating wasn't on, or if it was the chill of disappointment that was getting to her. Whatever it was, the empty rooms were telling their own tale. Her mother was not there, and after coaxing the central heating boiler into life, Kate switched on an electric fan heater in the sitting room and lay on the carpet in front of it to get warm.

As she gradually thawed out, her eyelids began to droop and just as she had decided that the sensible thing to do was to go to bed with a hot-water bottle, fever and exhaustion took over and she fell asleep.

* * *

She awoke when the light was switched on and as she lay with her eyes closed against the sudden brightness, Kate heard a deep voice say in surprise, 'So what have we here?'

It didn't have her mother's lighter tones, and with eyes bright and cheeks burning with a temperature that was still rising she sat upright and found herself gazing up into the dark hazel eyes of a man dressed in a smart suit, with shirt and tie to match.

'Who are you?' she croaked. 'Where is my mother?'

He gave a quirky smile. 'One thing I am not is the re-incarnation of Jack the Ripper, so there's no need to look so alarmed. Your mother is fine. That is presuming that you *are* the prodigal daughter. I'm Daniel Dreyfus and I'm staying here for the time being.'

'As a guest or a lodger?'

'I'm lodging here.'

'But why? Mum isn't in the habit of taking in lodgers.'

'So I believe, but she took pity on me. I've recently moved into this area and am having a house built. I needed somewhere to stay until it's ready to move into and there was nowhere available, so your mother made her kind offer.'

This was all she needed, Kate thought from her sitting position on the carpet. She was in no fit state to be coping with strangers. She'd come home seeking solace and had arrived with a virus of some sort. Her mother wasn't there and this stranger was living in the house.

'Where *is* my mother?' she asked.

'She's been called away because of an urgent message yesterday afternoon to say that your grandma has been taken ill. She set off immediately and wasn't here when you left your message last night. I only picked it up myself this morning, but you were already on your way when I tried to get in touch.'

'What's wrong with my gran?' she asked anxiously.

'Her heart, I think. Don't worry, she is recovering well. Your mother and I didn't have much time to talk. She phoned me at the surgery and asked me to hold the fort at this end. She had no idea that you were on your way.'

'What were you doing at the surgery?' she questioned, irritable now she was reassured that her mother and grandmother were OK. 'Are you sick? I'm fighting off some sort of bug of my own, so I can do without any other germs coming my way.'

The quirky smile was back. 'I work there. I'm the village doctor. Peter Swain, who was there before me, has retired. I took over the practice three months ago after a stint in the Middle East.'

What next? Kate thought wretchedly. Everything was going wrong. The really big catastrophe being Craig breaking off their engagement because he'd said he didn't want to be tied down, and then her finding out he was having an affair with her flatmate. She supposed she'd been too trusting and should have seen it coming, but it didn't hurt any less.

Then she'd picked up this virus thing. She who was never ill from one year's end to the next. Her gran was poorly too. It seemed as if it was her heart again. And to cap it all, this lodger person who was acting as if he owned the place was a doctor. She could do without *that*.

'I hope you're not using *my* room,' she said ungraciously, and began to get unsteadily to her feet.

'Of course not,' she heard him say smoothly, and that was the last thing she remembered.

Daniel caught Kate as she crumpled and was immediately aware of the fever in her. When he swept her up into his arms she lay limp and unresisting and he thought that with her short, spiky blonde hair and over-bright blue eyes, which were now closed, Kate looked nothing like her mother.

He carried her upstairs and opened the door of a bedroom that had been shut ever since he'd moved in. Pushing it back with his foot, he walked across to the bed and laid her gently on top of the covers. Then he went to forage in the top of the wardrobe for a blanket to put over her.

Kate was coming out of her faint and found herself in the same situation as before, looking up at him from a horizontal position. 'What happened?' she asked weakly.

'You fainted. So I carried you up here and laid you on the bed.'

She groaned. How embarrassing! What next?

'I want to check you over as you are certainly far from well. I'm going to get my bag out of the car so don't move,' he ordered.

If she hadn't felt so ghastly Kate would have argued. As it was she just lay there limply and waited for him to come back.

'How long since you've eaten?' he asked as he took her temperature.

'Er…yesterday.'

'No wonder you're feeling weak.'

'I kept vomiting.'

'Mmm. I see. Have you had this sort of thing before?'

'No. Never.'

'All right. So if you can manage to get undressed and slide under the covers, I'll go and sort out a hot-water bottle, a cup of tea and some toast. We'll see if you can keep that down, and then we'll try some paracetamol to bring your temperature under control.'

When he came back upstairs Kate was under the covers and shivering. She hugged the hot-water bottle to her thankfully. As she was sipping the tea and nibbling on the toast the phone in the hall downstairs rang and as he went to answer it she called after him, 'If it's my mother, don't tell her that I'm sick. She will have enough to cope with, looking after my gran.'

It wasn't her mother. The call was from Jenny Barnes, the mainstay of the reception desk at the surgery.

'Is everything all right, Dr Dreyfus?' she wanted to know. 'The waiting room is full and Dr Platt keeps sighing.'

'I'll be there in a few minutes,' he told her. 'I came back to get a medical book and found someone here who is not at all well.'

'You don't mean Ruth?'

'No. It's her daughter, who's arrived home unexpectedly and has a virus of some sort.'

'You mean Kate is back?' she exclaimed. 'She was a locum here for twelve months before she moved into hospital work. She's a sweetie.'

'Not at the moment she isn't,' he told her dryly as it registered that they were both in the same profession and she hadn't thought to mention it. In fact, she'd looked more put out than ever when he'd told her that he was in charge of the village practice.

'I'm needed at the surgery,' he told Kate when he went back upstairs and found her dozing after managing to get the tea and toast down. 'I'll be back as soon as I can and in the meantime stay put. I've brought your mobile up and have put it on the bedside table so that you won't have to get out of bed if your mother does ring.'

He paused in the doorway. 'Have you taken the paracetamol?'

'Yes,' she said meekly, and wished he wouldn't be so doctorish. Her heart was bruised and hurting. She didn't want to be taken over and organised. She wanted to be comforted. But this Daniel Dreyfus person wasn't to know that, and when he came back she would remember her manners and thank him for looking after her. Someone, somewhere must be on her case to have sent a fellow doctor to her in her hour of need.

A tear rolled down her cheek but he wasn't there to see it. The man who'd taken over the village practice and moved in on her home ground was halfway down the stairs and wishing that Miriam Platt, the other GP at the surgery, would cheer up.

He'd inherited the fifty-year-old widow with the practice. Peter Swain, who was now retired, had asked him to keep her on, and he'd agreed to do so unless for any reason he found her unsuitable. She was a good doctor, but personality-wise she was depressing. The slightest thing to go wrong had her sighing and he wished she would lighten up.

Miriam worried him. He wished she would talk to him. Tell him why she was always in such low spirits. The practice revolved around the two of them and if she had any problems that he could help with, he would be only too pleased.

He was aware that they needed another doctor, that they were short-staffed, and that his absence this afternoon wouldn't have gone down well with Miriam. But he couldn't have left that poor girl in the state she was in. For one thing, he liked Ruth Barrington. She was a pleasant, kindly woman, and for her sake as much as anything he'd stayed to sort her daughter out.

Ruth had been asked by her old friend Peter if she could accommodate the new doctor until his house was ready. She'd agreed and he was enjoying some good food and the pleasure of living in Jasmine Cottage for the time being.

He'd known that Ruth had a daughter somewhere and had sensed that she was concerned about her in some way, but she hadn't said why and he hadn't expected her to confide her anxieties to a stranger.

And now the daughter had appeared. Whether she was back for good, or just visiting he didn't know. But Kate hadn't been overjoyed to find him established in her mother's house, even though he'd explained that it was a temporary arrangement.

He was approaching the surgery where Miriam was moaning and patients were waiting to be seen, so she was going to have to sort herself out until his working day was over.

'So is Kate all right?' Jenny asked the moment he appeared.

'No. Not really,' he told her. 'I would say that it's some sort of virus she's got, and as we all know it is usually a case of keeping the temperature down and letting it run its course.'

'Does Ruth know she's poorly?' Jenny asked, not letting go until she had the full story.

'She's at her mother's in Newcastle-on-Tyne. The old lady has been taken ill, too. So I'm in charge at this end.'

As she passed over the notes of those who had come to consult him, Jenny said, 'Is there anything I can do to help with Ruth being away?'

He smiled, admiring how the villagers were always ready to rally round when needed. No one would be left to suffer alone in this place. He was amazed at the community spirit, but he had a feeling that on this occasion the patient would want to be left alone.

'Er...no, not at the moment. Thanks just the same,' he told her. 'Kate just seems to want to sleep.' With that, he went into his room and buzzed for his first patient before Miriam had a chance to cast her frowns upon him.

As he waited, he recalled how the local people had been wary of him at first. Peter had been their doctor for as long as some of them could remember. But they'd had time to get to know him and now they had his measure, knew him to be competent and briskly kind.

If any of the women patients wondered why such a presentable member of the opposite sex had arrived in their midst with no obvious family ties, they were left to ponder. Daniel was like his landlady. He kept his own counsel in matters close to his heart.

Patients came and went, some only mildly suffering, and others in dire distress. Now Millie from the chemist's was sitting opposite him. She was fighting breast cancer and needed a mastectomy because it had come back in a more serious form after a long remission.

'Would I have a better chance if I had them both removed?' she asked anxiously.

'Only the oncologist can advise you on that, Millie,' he

told her gently, 'and remember there is a chance that having the one mastectomy might be sufficient to give you a clean bill of health for a long time, maybe even permanently.'

'And it might not,' she reminded him. 'I'd rather go the whole way now, instead of wishing I had.'

'Have they given you a date?' Daniel asked.

'No. Not yet, but they've told me it will be soon. I wanted a word with you first before I approached them about a double mastectomy.'

'It is a difficult decision for you to make.'

She shook her head. 'Not really. If it gives me a few more years, it will be worth it.' She gave a watery smile. 'At least I won't feel lopsided.'

'So what does your husband say, Millie?'

'All he cares about is that I get better.'

'So have a word with the oncologist and see what he says.' Daniel advised patiently.

'It's a she,' Millie explained.

'Fine. You may find it easier to explain your feelings to another woman.'

As the numbers in the waiting room dwindled and the clock ticked on, Daniel wondered how his patient at Jasmine Cottage was feeling. She was far from well and somewhat disgruntled, but he sensed that her disappointment at finding her mother missing was mostly to blame for her lack of cordiality, as well as discovering that she hadn't got the house to herself.

But she couldn't have it both ways. At least he'd been there to look after her when she'd fainted and afterwards. And if she wasn't happy about him staying at Jasmine Cottage, he would have to keep a low profile while she was there and hope that it wouldn't be for long.

'I'm sorry I was delayed earlier,' he said to Miriam as they were clearing up at the end of the day. 'Ruth's daughter arrived home unexpectedly and she wasn't at all well. She fainted and I couldn't leave her until I was sure she would be all right.'

'I see,' she said distantly. 'It was just that we *were* rather busy.'

'Yes, I know. We need another doctor and I'm going to sort it the first chance I get.'

He didn't know how at that precise moment, but there were always young graduates keen to go into general practice, or more experienced doctors needing to relocate for family or other personal reasons.

It had been hectic since he'd taken over, but now everything was settling down and with another doctor in the practice he might find time to explore the Cheshire countryside.

One of the best things to happen to him since he'd become part of the rural community had been staying at Ruth Barrington's. He'd bought a piece of land down by the river and was having a detached house built on it. But it was going to be a matter of months before it was ready, and while that was going on he was happy and grateful to be based at Jasmine Cottage, or at least he had been until today.

It was half past six when he pulled up on the drive and as he let himself in there was no sound coming from anywhere in the house, so it seemed as if Kate might be asleep once more.

He knocked gently on her bedroom door and when there was no reply he pushed it open slowly. The bed was empty and he could hear the shower running in the en suite, so it seemed as if she was feeling better. But what had he advised? He'd told her to stay where she was. If she'd fainted in the shower it could have had serious consequences.

However, it appeared that she hadn't as at that moment she appeared draped in a towel, with feet bare and hair flat and damp against her head.

When she saw him standing there she clutched the towel more tightly around her and said defensively, 'I know what you said, but I felt so hot and sticky, and I'm not feeling so bad now. Whatever I've picked up must have reached its peak when I fainted.'

He shrugged. 'If you say so, and as we are both in the same line of business, I'm sure you know what's best for you, so I'll leave you to it.'

'Don't go,' she said quickly.

'Why? I'm hungry. Your mother told me to help myself to whatever I found in the fridge or the freezer. So I'm about to investigate. You can join me if you like, but don't feel you have to.'

'Would you just let me get a word in?' she protested, and he became silent.

'I want to apologise for my rudeness when you found me asleep in front of the heater, and also to say thanks for looking after me when I fainted. I don't usually behave in such a manner.' She sighed. 'My excuse is that I've just had to cancel my wedding. Over the last few weeks I've been going through the process of calling it off and it has been a distressing nightmare. But it is done now and I've come home to live for the time being.'

'I'm sorry to hear that,' he said quietly, and wondered

what she would say if he told her he knew the feeling. But there were lots of different reasons for calling weddings off, and he could bet that his wasn't the same as hers. 'Was it to take place here in the village?'

She shook her wet blonde head. 'No. My fiancé wanted us to be married abroad in St Lucia.'

'So a lot of your friends here would have been disappointed.'

'Yes. It wasn't my idea. But I was in love and…' She tailed off.

'Quite so,' he said, and turned to go. The conversation was bringing back painful memories that he could only cope with when he was alone.

'I'll put some clothes on and join you shortly, if that's all right,' she said hesitantly, with the feeling that she'd said the wrong thing again, but this time she didn't know what it was.

'I said it was, didn't I?' This time he did go, down the stairs and into the kitchen.

He was putting two plates of fish pie, peas and new potatoes on the table when she appeared hesitantly in the doorway, wearing a pink long-sleeved top and worn blue jeans, her blonde hair now dry. He had been feeling rather guilty about the way he had spoken to her upstairs and, seeing her now, looking so wary, he offered her a smile.

'Come and sit down,' he said, hoping he sounded more friendly. 'Did your mother phone while I was out?'

She relaxed a little, came in and sat down. 'Yes. Just after you'd gone. She was surprised to know I'm back home and sorry she wasn't here to greet me. Gran has had a quite severe angina attack and at the moment is in hospital. So Mum won't be returning until she is sure that all is well with her, and if there is any doubt about it she's going to bring her here to live. It's handy, having four big bedrooms.'

'Yes. Especially when one of them is being occupied by the lodger,' he commented dryly. 'Did you tell her that we've met?'

'Er…yes. She seems to think very highly of you and even more so after I told her how you'd looked after me.'

He nodded imperceptibly and for a while they ate in silence, both enjoying the tasty meal. Then Daniel spoke again.

'So why didn't you tell me that you're in medicine too?'

Kate shrugged. 'At the moment that's in the past. I was a doctor in A and E at a hospital down south. We both were. Craig, my fiancé, worked there too. But a few weeks ago the unit was transferred to another area where they had their own staff waiting to take over, which left some of us without jobs. I could have moved to another department, I suppose, like he did, but I left as a protest at the closure of a busy A and E centre.'

'So it would seem that life hasn't been treating you very well of late.'

'No. It hasn't. I wasn't the one who called off the wedding. He had been the one keen to get married. Then suddenly he didn't want to be tied down…to me, that was. He'd switched his affections to my flatmate.'

'I'm sure that you must feel you're well rid of him.'

She smiled, showing even white teeth, and he thought how it transformed her face. So far she'd been scowling most of the time, but now he was seeing her as someone who would be quite something if she smiled more…in spite of the hairstyle.

'I didn't at first. That kind of thing makes one feel so unwanted and unlovable, but I'm getting there.'

'I'm sure you are,' he said with a smile of his own, and thought that this girl had some spirit. It was a shame that some low-life had tried to quench it. "Perhaps when you are fully recovered we can drink a toast to your continuing return to good health and a future spent with people who won't let you down?'

'Hmm. That would be lovely. So maybe you could tell me what's happening at the surgery? Peter Swain has gone now, hasn't he?'

'Yes. But Miriam remains and I think she disapproves of me.'

'Why, for goodness' sake? Though thinking back to when I was there, it didn't take much for her to start sighing and rolling her eyes.'

He laughed. 'Nothing has changed, except that I'm in charge now and as new people are moving into the area our list of patients is getting bigger all the time.'

'Yes, it will be,' she agreed. Suddenly a wave of tiredness swept over her. Getting to her feet, she said apologetically, 'I think that maybe I left my bed a bit too soon. I'm not going to faint again,' she told him as he eyed her in concern. 'I just suddenly feel very tired.'

'That will be the after-effects of you having had such a high temperature. Do go back to bed by all means and I'll look in on you later to make sure you are all right. We can have the wine another time.'

She nodded and got up from the table, pausing in the doorway. 'I'm sorry I'm being such a drag, Dr Dreyfus,' she said.

He smiled. 'The name is Daniel, and none of us can

help being ill at some time or another, as we doctors well know, so don't give it another thought. You're probably run down after all the stress you've been under, and would have thrown the virus off at another time.'

As she went slowly up the stairs, Daniel was again wishing he hadn't been so brusque with her when he'd come back from the surgery. On closer acquaintance, Kate seemed all right.

Before he settled down for the night himself he went to check on her and found her sleeping peacefully. Her forehead was cool, her pulse regular, and as he moved away from the bed she turned in her sleep and murmured the name of the man she'd been going to marry, which made him wonder if she really had written him out of her life.

When he woke up the next morning he could smell bacon grilling and when he went downstairs Kate was setting the table for breakfast.

'My turn,' she told him as toast popped up in the toaster and the kettle came to the boil.

'So am I to take it that you are feeling better?' he asked.

'Mmm. Much. I'm going to start unpacking when we've had breakfast and I'm going to put the washing machine on, so if you have anything that needs washing, leave it out.'

'And what are you going to do after that?'

'Take a wedding dress to the charity shop in the village.'

'Surely someone else could do that for you. It's bound to be painful. I'll take it for you if you like.'

She was staring at him in amazement, unaware that for

him it would not be the first time. But on a previous occasion the dress hadn't been despatched with such haste and it had been returned to the shop from where it had been bought.

'I can't let you do that,' she protested. 'Mrs Burgess, who's in charge of the place, would have it on the grape-vine almost before you'd left the shop that you had brought in a wedding dress. What interpretation she and her helpers would put on that, I shudder to think.'

He was laughing. 'So why don't we set them a puzzle?'

'If you're sure.'

'Sure I'm sure, but are *you* sure that you and what's-his-name, Craig, aren't going to get back together?'

'That's not going to happen,' she said flatly. 'I've learnt my lesson. From this day forward I will only ever marry someone who can't live without me, and I can't live without him. And if I never find him I'll stay single. I think I was in love with love more than I was with Craig.'

'So where is the dress?'

'Upstairs in a big box. I'll go and fetch it.'

He must be insane, Daniel thought wryly after she'd gone to get it. Offering to take her brand-new wedding dress to the second-hand shop. It would be like turning the knife in him again, and what would Ruth think when she came home? That he ought to mind his own business. Or that he should have suggested to Kate that she sell it, being currently unemployed.

Why was he getting involved in her affairs anyway? They'd only met the previous day and hadn't exactly hit it off to begin with. He had enough to concern himself about without worrying over a jilted bride. Running the practice and keeping an eye on the builders working on his house down by the river, for a start.

But there was something about Kate that was reaching out to him and it wasn't because she was his type. Far from it. Lucy had been his type, but the after-effects of a brain tumour had taken her from him only days before their wedding, so he did understand how it felt to have one's future wiped away. In his case it had been the cruel fates that had broken his heart, not a cheating partner.

Kate was back with the box that had the dress in it. Ashen-faced but determined. As he took it from her she said, 'Thanks for taking it. I seem to have been putting on your good nature from the moment we met, and I know I'm pushing it, but I wonder if I could ask one more favour of you.'

'It depends what it is.'

'From what you were saying last night, it appears that you could do with another doctor in the practice. I have worked there before, and I do need a job.'

As soon as the words were out she wished she could take them back. His expression said it all. She *was* pushing it. Pushy was how she was coming over to him. She could tell.

'I'll have to think about it,' he said levelly. 'It is something I've been considering, but I'm not sure if I'm quite ready to act on it.' And carrying the big cardboard box in front of him, he went and got into his car and at the bottom of the drive pointed it in the direction of the charity shop.

CHAPTER TWO

WHEN he'd gone, Kate slumped down on to the sofa and gazed bleakly into space. Whatever had possessed her to ask such a thing of him on such short acquaintance? Had she expected him to jump at the chance of employing her when he had no way of knowing how proficient she was?

Having worked in the practice in the past, she had the experience, but Daniel hadn't seen her in action. It wouldn't be easy to look him in the eye when they next met. She'd been on the receiving end of his good nature since the moment he'd found her on the carpet in front of the electric heater. He'd even offered to take the wedding dress that she hoped never to see again to the charity shop, and now he must be thinking she was taking advantage.

The day stretched ahead, long and miserable, and she wished her mother was home to offer comfort.

That was a bolt from the blue! Daniel was thinking as he drove towards the main street of the village, Ruth's daughter asking to be taken into the practice. It had taken him by surprise and he'd fobbed her off, thinking as he did so that Kate wasn't backward at coming forward. He supposed that her life was in turmoil at present and she was seeing a job at the practice as a means of sorting out one part of it at least.

But when he took someone on it was going to be done properly with an in-depth interview, references and the rest. Not after a cosy little chat with his landlady's daughter. And if she was the right person for the job, then he would hire her. However, he also knew that the thought of working with Kate had unsettled him more than he wanted to admit.

After he'd lost Lucy he had decided that love and pain walked hand in hand and he couldn't go through that terrible kind of loss ever again. It was a defeatist attitude. He knew it. But it was why he steered clear of women and relationships. He didn't want Kate becoming any more entangled in his life than she was already.

The charity shop where Mrs Burgess ruled the roost was looming and, parking outside, he picked up the big cardboard box and went in. When he laid it on the counter and opened the top flaps of the box, there was a flurry of interest amongst staff and early morning customers alike, and someone said, 'It's beautiful. Just look at the lover's knots along the scalloped hemline. Who did it belong to?'

'An acquaintance,' he explained, having no desire to depart from the truth.

'It looks as if it's never been worn,' someone else said, and he shrugged noncommitally and wondered if Kate was making a mistake in getting rid of it so fast, though he understood that the dress was a reminder of how her hopes and dreams had been shattered.

Leaving them still admiring it, he drove to the surgery, intending to forget the jilted bride for a while as he concentrated on the needs of his patients.

As he was passing through Reception Jenny collared him, wanting to know how Kate was. 'Improving,' he told her. 'But I've told her to stay put and keep warm.'

Later on in the morning Mrs Giles brought her young son in for Daniel to see. The child was jerking his neck uncontrollably and his mother said anxiously, 'I've brought Billy to see you because of his neck.'

Daniel was on his feet and round their side of the desk before she'd finished speaking.

'How long has he been like this?' he asked, observing the neck movements keenly.

'He had a really bad sore throat last week,' Linda Giles said uncomfortably, 'and then he started twitching. His brothers and sisters keep laughing at him. But I thought I'd better bring him in to be looked at.'

'It is a good job you did,' he told her as he gently examined her son. 'Why didn't you bring him into the surgery when he had the inflamed throat?'

She shrugged. 'I gave him some Friar's balsam on a spoon with some sugar and it didn't seem as bad after that.'

Daniel frowned. 'Friar's balsam is a very old remedy, and in some cases is sufficient to clear up a sore throat, but what your son had would have been much worse than that,' he explained. 'He should have been seen by a doctor.'

The Giles family lived in an old tumbledown house at the top of the road that led to the circle of peaks that surrounded the village. There were five children in all and though Linda Giles did her best she never seemed to be on top of things.

'Why? Is it the sore throat that's making him twitch?' she wanted to know.

Daniel nodded. 'It could be.' Turning to Billy, he said, 'Can you hold your hands out in front of you for me, Billy, like this?' He showed him, with palms facing downward.

The child, who seemed to have a better idea of what was going on than his mother, obeyed, and Daniel saw what he didn't want to see. The fingers were curling backwards, and he knew he was seeing a case of Sydenham's chorea.

'Have you ever heard of St Vitus' dance?' he asked Mrs Giles. 'That's the common name of the illness that I think your son might be suffering from, which is rheumatism of the central nervous system. It's hardly heard of in this day and age but it can occur very rarely. I'm going to get Billy seen by a neurologist as soon as possible to see if I am right. In the meantime, take him home, put him to bed, keep him warm and give him the antibiotics that I'm going to prescribe for his throat.'

'I can't take him home. I'm on school dinners,' Linda protested. 'I've been taking him with me while he's been poorly.'

'Forget school dinners until he has been seen by the neurologist,' he told her firmly. 'The only thing that will stop the body movements getting worse is bed rest and sedation and I am not going to prescribe anything like that until a firm diagnosis has been made. So please do as I say.'

At last Mrs Giles seemed to realise the seriousness of the situation and she took Billy's hand in hers and led him out of the surgery. Daniel sighed and hoped that she would do as he had said.

He rang her later in the morning and told her he'd arranged an appointment with a neurologist for the following day. 'It will be a home visit,' he told her. 'He will be coming to the house so don't let Billy out of bed until he's seen him.'

'Oh!' she wailed. 'Does he *have* to come here? I haven't had the chance to put the vac round for days what with one thing and another.'

'Don't worry. He's not coming to look at the house. He's coming to see Billy,' he said. And I'm pretty sure I know what he will say, he thought as he said goodbye and put the phone down.

He'd told Billy's mother that the neurologist wasn't going to be looking at the house, but damp living conditions and poor nourishment would be noted.

When they were getting ready to leave at the end of the day he said to Miriam, 'What experience do you have of Sydenham's chorea in a patient?'

She was reaching for her coat and collecting her belongings, anxious to be gone, and she replied, 'So far, none. I've heard of it, of course.' And before he could explain that he would like to discuss little Billy's case with her, she was off.

When he arrived back at Jasmine Cottage, Kate was ironing the clothes that she'd laundered earlier in the day and he said with a frown, 'You don't have to do mine. I'm quite capable of ironing my own things.'

'Yes. I'm sure you are,' she told him, 'but you are not going to tell me that my mum doesn't do your ironing. I know her too well for that.'

'Yes. Ruth does do my washing and ironing. It was part of the deal when I moved in.'

'And so I'm taking her place.'

'So it would seem,' he commented dryly.

This sort of domestic scene was the very thing he wanted to avoid, he thought as he went upstairs to change out of the suit he'd worn at the surgery.

He didn't want this forced intimacy to become too cosy.

To begin with, Kate was too forthright and pushy. The absolute opposite of how Lucy had been. She had been gentle and amenable, with long silky hair and a piquant face. Life without her was an empty thing. Yet the woman downstairs ironing his shirts wasn't to blame for that. It was just that he didn't want any more complications in his life than he had already.

There was the business of her mentioning the vacancy at the surgery. The more they were thrown together the more she might see it as a reason for him to offer it to her, and he wasn't going to be manipulated.

They had a meal of sorts. Eating together at the kitchen table, pizza and a fruit flan that Ruth had put in the freezer. Short of being downright rude there was no way he could have avoided it. But once they'd cleared away he said, 'I'm going upstairs for a while to unwind. If I don't see you later, sleep well.'

Once in his room he lay down on top of the bed and picked up a book that he'd half read, but he couldn't settle into it. He felt restless and it was all because of Kate downstairs, who, if she had something to say, came out with it.

She had barged into his life just a short time ago and

ever since he'd felt as if his organised existence was being threatened. Yet Kate was vulnerable too in her own way. Trying to cope with being surplus to requirements for some low-life who had strung her along. She didn't deserve that.

She'd got the message, Kate thought when he'd gone. In a roundabout sort of way he was telling her to keep her distance. That enough was enough, and she couldn't blame him.

If she needed employment it was up to her to look for it instead of expecting it to be handed to her on a plate. But she was going to have to move out of the area if Daniel didn't want her in the practice.

She glanced through a magazine, watched some television half-heartedly, and finally decided to go to bed for lack of anything else to do. The days were stretching ahead emptily and she wished that Gran was better and her mother was home.

Ruth had never liked Craig. She'd thought he had a wandering eye and sadly she hadn't been wrong.

They'd drifted into a relationship, working long hours together, snatching quick meals. Talking shop sometimes, and at others letting the close environment they worked in shut out everyone else, so that it had been as if there had only been the two of them.

The odd thing was at this troubled time in her life the fates had sent another man into it, and the more she saw of Daniel the more Craig was becoming a shadowy figure. Yet she knew nothing about the GP who had taken Peter Swain's place in the village's health centre.

He was far too attractive for the women he met to

overlook deep hazel eyes and hair as dark as ebony curling neatly above his ears, yet he was alone and seemingly un-attached.

Surely he must have someone, somewhere who cared for him. A wife or a partner, a mother, or a sister. Or was the house he was having built by the river just for himself?

One thing was sure. She wasn't going to ask him. She'd already floored him twice in one day by her deter-mination to give away the wedding dress and almost in the same breath asking him about the vacancy at the practice. It was more than likely that he thought she wasn't exactly broken-hearted if she was job-hunting two days after her arrival and disposing of the dress that must have meant a lot to her at the same time.

She kept her tears for when she was alone in the dark hours of the night. The feeling of not being wanted hurt so much that she had to push it to the back of her mind when she was with Daniel in case she made a fool of herself. The last thing she wanted was for him to feel that she was looking for a shoulder to cry on.

Getting up off the sofa, she began to walk slowly upstairs, having given up on seeing him again before morning, but as she reached the landing the door of his bedroom opened and he was framed there, dressed in a thick sweater and jeans with a sheepskin jacket over the top.

'Hi,' he said warily. 'You aren't going to bed, are you?'

'Yes,' she told him flatly. 'There doesn't seem much else to do.'

'It's only half past nine.'

'So?'

She looked pale and lost and he weakened, saying,

'I'm going down to the pub for an hour. Do you want to come?'

He couldn't believe he'd said it when the words were out. This wasn't keeping Kate at a distance. Her expression had brightened but she was hesitating.

'That would be nice,' she said, 'but I hope that everyone doesn't start asking questions about why I've come back to live. I presume my mother will have told some people that I'm engaged and they'll be curious because it wasn't someone local, but I don't want to suddenly be the focus of attention.' Kate sighed. 'It hurt a lot to have my trust betrayed. The fact that I won't be wearing the wedding dress or honeymooning abroad is disappointing, but delightful as those things are, they're just the trappings of a wedding. It's knowing that the person you're marrying can be trusted to love and cherish you that matters. With Craig that was never going to happen, so I suppose I should consider myself to have had a lucky escape, but it doesn't make the pain go away.'

'I can believe that,' Daniel said gravely, finding himself wishing that he knew her well enough to offer comfort. 'But, Kate, you will have to face the people around here some time, so why not get it over and done with?'

She smiled for the first time since they'd met on the landing. 'Yes. Why not? At least I'll have you for moral support.'

'You will indeed,' he promised, and thought that it was a long time since he'd felt so protective over anyone, but he wasn't sure if he wanted it to be like that.

A diversion was called for and, remembering little Billy Giles, he asked her, 'Have you ever seen or treated anyone with Sydenham's chorea, rheumatism of the central nervous system?'

She frowned thoughtfully. 'I know what it is, but I've never treated anyone with it. Although I do believe I once saw someone whose life had been blighted by it.'

'So go and get your coat and make sure that you wrap up warm. It isn't long since you were ill, so don't take any chances, and you can tell me about it while we're walking to the pub.'

Kate nodded and went into her room to quickly get ready while Daniel waited downstairs. Then they stepped out of the house and began the pleasant walk towards the pub.

'So why are you asking about Sydenham's chorea?' Kate asked immediately. 'You haven't got a patient with it, have you?'

'I might have, and it's very much on my mind. A young boy who from the sound of it has had a severe throat infection, came to see me this morning with his mother. He was making uncontrollable neck movements all the time and I suspect that it is the jolly old St Vitus' dance as it used to be called way back.'

'What makes you think so? The twitching of the neck?'

'Yes, that, and also what happened when I tested him in the same way that a neurologist once did on a patient that I'd sent to him with the same kind of problem.'

'What sort of test?' she asked, and he thought at that moment she wasn't his landlady's daughter or the jilted bride, she was the doctor first and foremost, tuned in, keen to know. Miriam could take a lesson from Kate.

'When the boy stretched his hands out in front of him palms down, his fingers curled backwards. I've tried it with my hands, and if you try it with yours you'll find that it is almost impossible to make them do that. So simple, but so illuminating, though I never found out what it actually revealed. But it will be interesting to see what happens tomorrow.'

'That's interesting,' she commented. 'That someone could be diagnosed in such a way.'

'I know, but that is how it was then. They may have other ways of making a diagnosis now. So tell me about this person that you saw.'

'It was a man in a big department store. His whole body was on the go all the time, making exhausting sweeping movements. Some people were laughing at him, but I just felt so sorry for him I could have wept. I thought at the time that it might have been Sydenham's chorea, but had no way of knowing if it was, short of asking him, and he was having enough to cope with without that. It comes from a streptococcal throat infection, doesn't it, and poor living conditions?'

'Yes, and Billy Giles lives in a damp old house. They are a big family and I don't somehow think they live off the fat of the land, even though the father works on a farm. Immediate and prolonged bed rest is essential to prevent the damage to the nervous system progressing, so I bundled him off home to bed and have arranged for a home visit from a neurologist tomorrow.'

'I'll be very interested to know what happens,' she said. 'Would it be possible for me to see Billy, so that if ever I do come up against it I will be better informed than I am now?'

'Yes, of course,' he said immediately. 'I'll be visiting him regularly once it is sorted and I'll take you with me if you like.'

He was weakening, Daniel was thinking. He knew it. But her kind of enthusiasm was what he was looking for in the practice. Miriam was a good doctor, but he'd never found her prepared to go the extra mile.

'Maybe you could come down for an interview,' he said as the pub came into sight, and as her expression brightened he thought that Kate was going to be renewing her acquaintance with the villagers inside The Poacher's Rest with a bit more sparkle than when they'd left the house.

'Hello, there, Daniel,' Michael Grimshaw, the landlord, said when they appeared, and, on seeing who was with him, 'Kate! Nice to see you. Are you just visiting, or back for good?'

Before she had the chance to answer someone called from across the room, 'So when's the wedding, Kate? We're always ready for a chance to dress up in the village, especially when it's for one of our own.'

Daniel cast a quick glance at his companion. Was he ever going to be free of the feeling of responsibility he'd had for her from the very moment of their meeting? he wondered. What was Kate going to say to that?

The sparkle had gone as quickly as it had come, but she was totally composed as she announced for the benefit of anyone listening, 'The wedding preparations are on hold at the moment. We're spending some time apart, but I will bear in mind that you would like me to be married here when the occasion arises.'

As they sat down with their drinks he murmured. 'Well done and very subtle. I'm proud of you. That took some pluck. It should give you some breathing space and delay any surmises about the wedding dress for the time being.'

She flashed him a watery smile. 'Thanks for being

with me. It did make it easier. At least I've been able to give a hint of things to come.'

'You have indeed, and now relax for a while, Kate. What shall we talk about?'

The smile was still there. "Sydenham's chorea?'

'No. We've given that enough of an airing until I have some results on young Billy.' He sighed. 'It's been a week of coming into contact with some very unfortunate people, but of course that's the doctor's lot.

'I had an anxious young woman consult me who is fighting breast cancer and is facing a mastectomy. She's considering having both breasts removed to give herself a better chance and wanted my opinion.'

'What did you advise?'

'That she see the oncologist and get an opinion from her. She is under the hospital and I don't know enough about her case to tell her what to do, but I could see sense in what she was contemplating.'

'It makes one's own troubles seem small compared to that kind of problem, doesn't it?' Kate said sombrely.

'Hmm. But they don't go away because of it, do they?'

She glanced at him curiously. 'You don't come over as having problems Although I do sense that you are alone. Do you not have any family?'

'If you mean am I married, or in any other kind of re- lationship, the answer is no.'

'Amazing,' said Kate, wondering why such an attrac- tive man was on his own.

'What do you mean?' asked Daniel levelly, as he sipped his drink.

'Just that lots of women would see you as their dream man.'

He laughed, but there was no mirth in it. 'Really? Well, I'm sure that you won't get any of those sorts of ideas. Though saying that, I know how the minds of people on the rebound can work.'

As she was about to voice an indignant protest he went on, 'I'm afraid that my life is not an open book, like yours. Some of its pages will stay closed for ever. Both my parents are dead. I had a fantastic childhood and would have wanted the same for any children I might have. But we don't always get what we want, do we?'

'So are the closed pages about your parents?' Kate asked, rather annoyed about his assumption that she could be some sort of desperate woman on the rebound.

'No,' he said abruptly. 'They are not, and I think we should be making a move. If you can lie in bed in the morning, I can't.'

'What about my interview?' Kate asked nervously.

'Leave it with me. After the house calls and before the late surgery would be a good time, but I'll have to check with Miriam so that she will be available to join us. I don't want to go over her head in this.'

As they walked home in the quiet night beneath a sky full of stars Daniel said, 'Do you think you might find working at the practice a bit tame after a busy A and E department?'

'I didn't before,' she told him. 'General practice might move at a slower pace, yet it's just as challenging in its own way.'

Kate couldn't help but feel hopeful. But she told herself she wasn't there yet. There was nothing to say that she was the only person he had in mind for the position, and what about Miriam? Would she want her on the staff?

That night she dreamt about the wedding dress. That she'd gone to the wardrobe and it was hanging there unused and unwanted. In the dream she'd cried out in dismay and Daniel had come dashing in to see what was wrong.

'You said you'd taken it to the charity shop!' she'd sobbed.

'What? The wedding dress? I did!' he'd cried, and when she looked again it had gone.

She must have been crying out in her sleep because his voice broke into the dream and she woke up. He was outside her door, asking if she was all right. Getting slowly out of bed, she padded across in her nightdress and opened the door.

'I was dreaming,' she told him. 'I'm sorry if I disturbed you.'

'It can't have been very pleasant from the sound of it.'

'It was about the wedding dress. I dreamt it was in the wardrobe and I thought it had come back to haunt me.'

'Well, we both know that's crazy, don't we?' he said calmly. 'Go back to bed and I'll go down and make you a drink. What would you like? Tea, coffee, hot chocolate?'

'Hot chocolate would be lovely,' she said awkwardly. 'I am really so sorry that I disturbed you.'

'You didn't. I was reading for a while. Otherwise I mightn't have heard you. You're not likely to put a cancelled wedding behind you without bad moments, you know. Just take it one day at a time.'

She nodded meekly. 'Yes. I will.'

It would have been their visit to the pub that had triggered the dream, she thought when he'd gone downstairs.

They'd passed the charity shop on the way and she'd been acutely aware that inside it was her wedding dress.

She gratefully accepted the hot chocolate Daniel soon brought up to her. About to leave, he asked from the doorway of her bedroom, 'Has your mother been in touch today?'

'Yes. She rang this morning and sends her regards.'

'Any signs of her coming home?'

'Not so far,' she told him with a feeling that he might be asking for various reasons. One of them being that he would be happy to pass her and her problems back into her mother's keeping.

'So your gran is no better?'

'Mum says she's improving, but has quite a way to go yet.'

'The main thing is that she's recovering. It must be a relief for you both, and now, if you promise not to have any more strange dreams, I'll go and get some sleep myself, and will see you in the morning.'

'Thanks once again for putting up with me,' she said, her blue eyes appealing.

'Don't mention it,' he replied dryly, and went to try and forget her for a few hours.

The next morning he said to Miriam, 'I'm thinking of interviewing Kate Barrington for the position of a third doctor in the practice, and I'd like you to be there.'

'Really?' she said stiffly. 'Since when?'

'Since I have found her to be an intelligent and knowledgeable young doctor. Do you have any objections?'

'If it reduces my workload, no. She has worked here before, you know.'

'Yes. So I believe. What was she like then?'

'Young, enthusiastic. Eager to learn, I suppose.'

'So why didn't she stay?'

'The pull of hospital health care where she has been employed until very recently, I believe.'

'Yes, that's right,' he agreed, 'but I think that Kate has given up on that and wants to be more home-based. So how about I ask her to come in tomorrow after we've finished the home visits?'

'Yes, I suppose so,' she said in her usual flat tones, and went to start her day.

That was one hurdle crossed, he thought when she'd gone. He had not been sure of how Miriam would react, but it seemed as if Kate had been highly suitable when she'd worked in the practice before, so she was already halfway to being taken on. He just wished that she was of a similar age to Miriam and just as unexciting, then she wouldn't take over his thoughts so much.

He rang her in his lunch-hour to tell her about the interview time. She'd still been asleep when he'd left, but now she was up and about and happy to know that things were moving.

'What did Miriam say?' she wanted to know.

'She seemed to approve of the idea.'

'Oh, good! I'll keep my fingers crossed, then, and, Daniel, whether you offer me the position or not, thank you for being so good to me.'

There was a moment's silence at the other end of the line and then he said stiltedly, 'Yes, well, thanks for that. The truth of the matter is that I've felt I owed it to your mother to look after you. Ruth has been very kind to me. You are very fortunate to have her in your life.'

When he'd replaced the receiver Kate wondered why she felt as if she'd been warned off. There was no reason why she should, but the feeling was there nonetheless. Maybe it was why Daniel was alone. There was something of the 'don't butt into my life' about him.

Yet he seemed to get on fine with her mother and the villagers seemed to all like him. Perhaps it was just her that he was wary of. But why? She certainly hadn't got any designs on him. Her heart was bruised and aching from what Craig had done to her. Yet, she thought with wry amusement, Daniel was the only man whose underwear she had ever laundered, though he'd made it clear at the time that he'd rather she hadn't.

She decided that tomorrow she wouldn't put a foot wrong. If nothing else, she would get a smile out of Miriam.

CHAPTER THREE

WHEN Kate arrived for the interview Daniel's first thought was, Wow! The young doctor from A and E was out to make a statement, he decided. With hair brushed into a smooth gold bob, light make-up accentuating her delicately boned features, and dressed in a smart black trouser suit with a white silk shirt and black leather shoes with medium heels, she looked more like a young executive than a country GP. It would be interesting to observe Miriam's reaction when she saw the prospective newcomer to the practice, he thought. As for himself, he just wished that Kate would stop weakening his resolve, though he had only himself to blame for that. He was the one who'd asked her to come for an interview in spite of not wanting to get too close to her.

But turning up looking so stunning wasn't going to get her the job. It would depend on how knowledgeable she was about general practice work. How much she remembered from when she'd been employed in the practice before, and most of all how good a doctor she was, though he would only discover that when he saw her in action.

He knew she wouldn't be short on enthusiasm. There

had been nothing lukewarm about her interest in young Billy Giles, who had now been seen by the neurologist and pronounced to be suffering from Sydenham's chorea.

Kate was that kind of person. He'd discovered in the short time he'd known her that there was nothing negative about her. The disposal of the wedding dress was proof of that, though he still wasn't sure that she should have been in such a rush, and he hoped that whoever bought it wouldn't be walking down the aisle of the village church in it.

When he glanced around Reception she was sitting there, waiting patiently for him to call her into his consulting room, but Miriam, who was usually back first from her house calls, hadn't yet returned and he wasn't going to start without her.

She arrived in due course. The interview commenced, and as it progressed Daniel knew he would be crazy not to take Kate into the practice. Her appointment would have to go through the usual channels with regard to admin, but he couldn't foresee any problems there. She was bright, intelligent and should be no mean performer after working in A and E for quite some time.

Even Miriam was smiling. Though that could be for a variety of reasons, self-preservation being top of the list, and maybe she was pleased at the thought of another woman doctor in the practice. He still had concerns about his colleague and wished she would open up to him about whatever it was that was making her so unhappy. Maybe she would confide in their third member once she'd settled in.

'I'll be in touch,' he told Kate when it was over.

She was smiling. 'In person, or through the post?'

'As we are more or less living on top of each other at the moment, I think I can safely say it will be in person.'

He could have told her on the spot that he wanted her in the practice, but he had to make sure that Miriam's smile was because she was in favour of Kate joining them, and that it wasn't for any other reason.

'Yes,' she said when his landlady's daughter had gone. 'If you're happy about taking Kate on, so am I.'

Still in her smart clothes, Kate was walking down the main street of the village about to do some food shopping while she was out. As she strolled along, uppermost in her mind was the interview that had just taken place, and when the window of the charity shop suddenly loomed up beside her she wasn't prepared for what she was about to see.

Totally unmissable in the centre, with lover's knots and pristine white satin arranged to the best of their ability by Mrs Burgess and her ladies, was her wedding dress.

She began to shake. All the bottled-up hurt and disappointment was hitting her with full force, and tears that so far hadn't seen the light of day began to pour down her cheeks.

The shop closed at four o'clock each day when the staff went home to their own devices, so her grief was unobserved from inside. But to Daniel, driving past in answer to a phone call from a home for the elderly a couple of miles out of the village, there was no mistaking the slender figure in the black trouser suit standing in mute distress where someone might come across her at any moment.

He pulled up quickly and was out of the car in a flash.

Taking her arm, he said gently, 'Get inside, Kate. I'll take you home. But I've got to answer a request for a home visit first. They've just been on the phone from Furzebank. One of their old folk is really poorly and they're very concerned.'

She nodded, wiped her eyes, blew her nose, and huddled down in the seat beside him as he drove off. When they reached the gates of a big stone house that had been converted into a home for the elderly, Daniel said in the same gentle tone, 'Kate, I did warn you that it could be a bit hasty, sending your dress to the charity shop so soon after your return to the village.'

Still without speaking, she nodded again and he thought that the smiling and confident interviewee of not so long ago was red-eyed and hurting and the same concern that he'd felt when they'd walked home from the pub was there.

He wanted to comfort her, hold her close, tell her that one day a man would come along who would love her as she deserved to be loved. Someone who wasn't wrapped around with memories of the past, and he, Daniel, would envy him.

He hadn't held a woman in his arms since he'd lost Lucy. That way he was able to keep to the commitment he had promised himself, so he just patted her hand and said anxiously, 'Promise me you won't budge while I'm in the home. I'll try not to be too long but can't be sure.'

'I'll be here,' she promised. 'Don't rush on my account, Daniel. Patients come before personal matters in the life of the GP during surgery hours.' And when he glanced at her sharply she managed a smile. 'I know I'm not a GP yet, but I'm hoping.'

It was Elizabeth Ackroyd, the oldest inmate of

Furzebank, that he'd been summoned out to see, and when he saw her Daniel's expression was grave. She had been a highly intelligent woman and still was to some degree in spite of her ninety years.

She had sacrificed the chance of marriage or a career to look after younger brothers and a sister when they'd lost their mother while only young, and she had outlived them all.

Elizabeth had been at Furzebank four years and until recently had been well and happy. Until an elderly widower that she had become very close to had died suddenly and the will to live had left her.

The first time Daniel had been called out to her, he hadn't been able to find anything organically wrong with her. Helen, the sister-in-charge, had nodded her agreement, and told him that Elizabeth had said to her that she'd found the love of her life seventy years too late, and that she would die of a broken heart.

Today Elizabeth was very poorly. Her pulse and heartbeat were irregular, her breathing laboured. But she looked peaceful enough, and he said to Helen, 'She might go during the night. Just keep her comfortable and try to get some liquids down if you can. Ring me if you need me, Helen, and I'll come straight away.'

'It won't be the same when she's gone,' she said regretfully. 'I thought Elizabeth would have seen a hundred. But love can be a painful thing, can't it? It can bring joy like no other, and it can also deprive life of its meaning.'

Daniel nodded. He wasn't going to disagree with that. He'd been there.

Kate was where he'd left her, as she had promised she would be, staring into space and taking little note of his presence in the car once more until he said, 'So aren't you going to ask me about the patient that I've just been to see? If I'm not around, you could be called out to her the next time.'

Slowly raising herself upright, she turned to face him and asked, 'Are you saying what I think you're saying?'

'Mmm. When can you start?'

'Oh!' she cried, with spirits lifting. 'Daniel, you are offering me the perfect antidote to keep the blues at bay. I'm sorry about earlier. It was the shock of seeing the dress in all its glory in the shop window. It was a bit like the dream I had. As if it had come back to haunt me. Love can be very hurtful sometimes, can't it?'

'Yes,' he agreed, and thought that made three of them who had come to that conclusion. Elizabeth, who had lost the will to live. He himself, who had been going in that direction when Lucy had died, until he'd taken himself in hand, and Kate, who from the sound of it might have had a lucky escape.

And now he was going to see her safely home before he went to take his share of the late surgery, and once that was over he hoped to find her still in a happier frame of mind than when he'd found her outside the charity shop.

Kate's rise in spirits was still in evidence when he returned to Jasmine Cottage in the early evening. He found her standing over the cooker poised to make ome-lettes and didn't know whether to be glad or sorry that she was organising their evening meal once more.

He knew that he ought to be grateful, and that it might be the last time she was available to have a meal ready when he got in as soon they would be equally busy with the affairs of the practice.

Offering her the position wasn't going to alter his intention of keeping their relationship impersonal, but he knew that he wasn't going to be able to stand by and do nothing during moments like those outside the charity shop when she needed him.

Kate was going to be like an enthusiastic and efficient breath of fresh air in the village's practice and *that* was what he was looking for. Hopefully working together would seem less claustrophobic than living in the same house.

Regarding that, he was just going to have to play it as it came. Be friendly but not too friendly, helpful but not too helpful, and in the meantime he was going to keep pushing the builder to get his house finished.

A phone call just as he was finishing his meal wiped every other thought from his mind. Lucy's only living relatives were her fifty-year-old father, Tom, and her eight-year-old brother Alex. Her mother had died some time previously from a similar illness to her daughter's and Tom was bringing Alex up on his own in a town in the Midlands.

Lucy had adored young Alex, who had come into the world when her mother had been menopausal, and he had been just five and a half years old when his big sister had been taken from them.

She'd said to him once as the illness had taken over her life, 'You'll help Dad with Alex if I don't get better, won't you, Daniel? It won't be easy for either of them.'

'You don't need to ask,' he'd whispered tenderly. 'Of course I will.' And had wondered how he would be able to bear being with her father and brother, while knowing that *she* was gone for ever.

But he'd kept his promise and gone to see them every couple of months, taking Alex out for the day to give Tom a break. He loved the child and saw him as the nearest he was ever going to get to having a family of his own.

Tom was coping brilliantly, having gone onto part-time hours with the building firm where he was employed so that he would be there during out-of-school times and holidays, and until a few moments ago Daniel had had no worries about them.

When Daniel heard Tom's voice at the other end of the line he thought that Lucy's father had rung for a chat, as he sometimes did, but he was wrong.

Tom rarely lost his cool, but today his voice was hoarse with anxiety and it soon became evident why.

'I need your help. Daniel,' he said. 'You are the only person I can ask.'

'What's wrong, Tom?' he questioned.

'I'm in hospital. I've had an accident at work and fractured both my knees. I'm going to need quite a bit of surgery over a period and could be here for a few weeks. I'm in A and E at the moment, waiting to go to Theatre to be put together again. I'm hoping that I'll have more luck than Humpty Dumpty,'

'Tom, I am sorry,' Daniel said, his voice full of concern for the man who had so nearly become his father-in-law.

'Tell me about it!' Tom groaned. 'I'm ringing to ask if you can have Alex until I'm mobile again.'

'Yes, of course,' Daniel said immediately. 'I'll do anything I can to help. Where is he now?'

'He's here with me, and Social Services have just

arrived to sort something out regarding his care while I'm in here. They're talking about fostering and it's breaking his heart. Doesn't want to leave me, which is not surprising as I'm all he's got.'

'You are not *all* he's got, Tom,' Daniel said steadily. 'He's got me. Will he let me bring him back here if I come for him now?'

'No problem,' he replied, his voice lifting with relief. 'When I said I was going to ring you he was all for it. I can't let him go to strangers, Daniel. He's had enough to cope with already in his young life.'

'Tell Social Services I'm setting off now,' he said. 'If the roads are quiet it should take me a couple of hours, and once we've been to your place to pick up some clothes and his toys, I'll bring him back here for as long as it takes.'

'Thanks. I knew I could count on you,' he said raggedly, and that was that.

Daniel put the phone down slowly, knowing that he'd just made a rash promise that he would keep, come hell or high water. But he didn't know how he was going to do it.

He was living in someone else's house as a lodger. He could hardly bring an eight-year-old boy to Jasmine Cottage, unannounced and without permission.

He'd left the dining table when Tom's call had come through and had taken it in the hall. When he returned to the dining room Kate observed him questioningly. 'I couldn't help overhearing,' she said, 'and it sounded like trouble.'

'It is,' he told her flatly. 'Someone I know is in hospital with two shattered knees and is going to be in there for some weeks. He's a widower with a young son and has asked me to look after him until he is well again.

'I'll be setting off for Gloucestershire in the next quarter of an hour and need to ask if it is all right if I bring him back here for the night. I know it's an imposition as you've already got me on the premises, but first thing in the morning I'll sort out somewhere else for Alex and I to stay. His father has asked me because there is no one else he could turn to.'

'Poor things,' she said softly, and in the next breath, 'You don't have to move out, Daniel. The little boy can have the smallest of the two guest rooms. We can look after him together. Just go and get him.'

He smiled. 'You are something else, Kate. Thank you. I hope that your mother won't mind when she hears about this.'

'Mum would only mind if I hadn't made the offer,' she told him calmly. 'So off you go, and while you're gone I'll get the room ready.'

It would be nice to have a child in the house, Kate thought as she put fresh sheets on the bed and found some pictures to adorn the walls which she'd had in her room when she was small. But the circumstances of it were sad.

Who were these people? she wondered. Daniel had just said it was someone he knew, which didn't sound like a relative, but the person obviously felt they could rely on him in a crisis.

He'd referred to the boy as Alex and in the absence of any toys in the house she found a fancy box and filled it with goodies, then wrote on the outside 'For Alex' and next to it she placed a glass of fruit juice.

It was one o'clock in the morning when Daniel's car pulled onto the drive and Kate was round at the passenger's side in a flash. As she opened the door a pair of sleepy blue eyes were fixed on her and a small voice asked, 'Are you Kate?'

'I am,' she told him with a smile, 'and you must be Alex.'

Daniel was watching them from the driving seat. 'We have one very tired boy here, Kate.'

'Come along, then,' she said gently, helping him out of the car. 'There's a nice bed waiting for you but, first, are you hungry, Alex?'

He shook his head and Daniel explained, 'He was starving, so we stopped at a service station on the motorway, and now all I think Alex wants is to go to sleep, isn't it?' he said, placing his arm around the boy's shoulders.

'Then come this way, both of you,' she said, and led the way to the room that was going to be Alex's for a time. 'I'll leave you to it now,' she told Daniel. 'I'm sure that Alex would rather you showed him where the bathroom is and helped him undress on his first night here. I'll see you both in the morning.'

When Kate had gone, sleepy though he was, Alex pointed to the box on the bedside table and said, 'Can I open it? My name is on it.' And when he lifted the lid he smiled for the first time since they'd left Tom at the hospital.

Bless you, Kate, Daniel thought. You deserve far better than that cheating fiancé of yours. You will be just what we need at the surgery for our small patients.

In another life he might have thought that she was just what *he* needed, but not in this one.

* * *

When Alex cried out for his dad in the night, Kate and Daniel almost bumped into each other on the landing in their haste to get to him. But she stepped back when she saw him and said with a smile, 'Great minds think alike, it would seem. I'll leave you to it.'

But he noticed that she didn't remove the wedge that she'd placed under her bedroom door to keep it open, and when he'd hushed Alex back to sleep he saw that she was propped up in bed reading a magazine.

'Go to sleep, Kate,' he said in a low voice. 'I'll keep my eyes and ears open.'

'All right,' she agreed, sinking back against the pillows, 'but who are they, Daniel—Alex and his father?'

'Can it wait until tomorrow?'

'Yes, I suppose so.' As he turned the light off she added, 'Was it only a few hours ago that you told me I was going to be doctor number three in the practice? It seems like a lifetime.'

'It's because a lot has happened since then,' he replied, and wondered how they were going to give an eight-year-old boy the loving care he was going to need and keep the practice running smoothly at the same time.

The next morning, while their young visitor was still sleeping, Kate went down to the kitchen and made a pot of tea with the intention of taking some up to Daniel if he was awake, but before she could do so he appeared looking somewhat heavy-eyed, and she observed him sympathetically.

'I take it that you didn't get much sleep,' she said.

'No, I didn't,' he admitted. 'I dozed off a few times but was loath to let myself get too comfortable in case Alex cried out again. The early hours of the morning were not a good time for a child to be taken to a strange house and put to bed in a strange room, but once he'd settled into a deep sleep I didn't hear a sound from him. The poor kid was exhausted.'

'So are you going to tell me what it's all about?' she asked as she poured the tea.

'I suppose so. I owe you that if for no other reason than the way you were so kind and caring with Alex last night. I am in contact with the boy and Tom, his father, because I was once engaged to Alex's older sister.'

Kate managed to hide her surprise. 'I see. But I take it that you didn't marry her.'

'No. I didn't marry Lucy. I was going to, but I didn't.'

She frowned. 'So you had a change of heart.'

'No. Neither of us changed our minds. We were very much in love, but circumstances did it for us. She died the week before we were due to be married. Lucy had a brain tumour.'

'Oh! How awful!' she gasped. 'How did you cope with something so dreadful?'

'For a long time not very well, I'm afraid. But in the end I just had to get a grip on my grief and get on with my life. I went to work abroad for a while, but the pain was still there no matter where I was, so when I came back I opted for the life of a country GP and so far have no regrets on that score.

'Her mother had died from the same thing as her daughter some years before, so when Lucy was taken it left just her father and young Alex. There were no other relatives, but they've been fine so far. Tom is a great father to the boy, and I've kept in touch because Lucy asked me to. So you know now why I couldn't refuse when he asked me to look after Alex. He calls me his Uncle Dan.'

Kate felt like weeping. Her own blighted engagement seemed as nothing compared to what had happened to Daniel. She had her answer now as to why he was alone. It was from choice. No one was ever going to replace Alex's big sister in the life of the man sitting opposite, and coming to that conclusion made her feel even more like weeping.

'You must see what happened to *my* marriage plans as trivial when you think back to what happened to yours,' she said, looking down at the place where her wedding ring would have rested.

'No! Not at all,' he said firmly. 'You had a raw deal. But, Kate, you are young and attractive. It won't be long before someone else wants to marry you and have children with you. What is happening to you now will just seem like a bad dream then.'

She wanted to tell him that getting to know him was the only thing that was making her life bearable, and if she did meet someone else he would have a hard act to follow after her having spent time with a man who'd stayed awake all night in case a small boy woke up in a strange house and wanted his dad.

While Kate's thoughts had been all about him, Daniel's mind had been moving on. 'I'll call in at the school some time today and ask if they are prepared to take in a temporary pupil in the middle of term,' he said. 'If Alex can start tomorrow, there is no reason why you shouldn't join us at the practice at the same time.'

'That would be great,' she enthused, 'just as long as he is at school and comes to the surgery afterwards. But I wouldn't mind putting it off for a while if you want me to so that I can be there for him until he's settled into his new surroundings.'

Daniel shook his head. 'No, Kate, I can't let you do that. Alex is my responsibility. Let's not make any decisions until I've spoken to the headmaster.'

'I've got today free,' she insisted. 'I could sort that out for you. He and I could go to the school and see the headmaster.'

'You are just too good to me,' he said with a smile, 'but Alex is in *my* care. I'll tell you what, though. We'll all three go to the school. How about that?'

'Yes!' She smiled. 'It's going to be lovely, having him around for a while, isn't it? He can ring his dad whenever he wants and we'll take him to see him at the weekends.'

'Which reminds me,' he said, 'Tom will be anxious to hear that Alex arrived here safely and that he is all right. When he's had some breakfast he and I will give him a ring. The poor guy has bone splintering in each of his knees so it's going to be metal plates and whatever else is needed to get him mobile again. It will be like he said, a big job.'

Having someone like Kate around would be just what Alex needed, he thought as he went upstairs to see if he was awake. She was ready to put her own affairs on hold because of his commitment to Tom and Alex, but he couldn't let her do that. It wouldn't be fair.

He'd noted that to her they were already a threesome with regard to Alex, and thought that not so long ago he would have been putting up barriers at the description, but now it had a comforting sound to it. It was good to have

Kate in his life. Without her the responsibility that he'd just taken on would be much more overwhelming.

When he reached the top of the stairs Alex was coming out of the bedroom, looking around him curiously and clutching the box of goodies that Kate had left for him the night before.

'Hi, Alex,' Daniel said breezily, as if it was the most natural thing in the world for them to be meeting on the landing, 'Are you ready for something to eat?'

Alex nodded and, still looking around him, asked, 'Where's Kate, Daniel?'

'In the kitchen, making breakfast and looking forward to seeing you again. I will have to go to the surgery today to look after my patients, but Kate will be here to keep you company, and at some part of the day the three of us are going to go to the village school to ask if they can find a place for you until your dad is better.'

'Do we have to?' he asked with a noticeable lack of interest.

'I'm afraid so. He won't want you to miss any of your schooling.'

'Can I talk to him?'

'Yes. Any time you like. But let's have breakfast first, shall we? Your dad might be with the doctors at this time of the morning.'

'Hello, there,' Kate said, directing a bright beam upon him. 'Has Daniel told you that you and I are going to explore the village today while he's looking after the poorly people?'

'Yes. What is there to see?' he asked doubtfully.

'There's the river, where we can fish when I'm not working,' Daniel told him. 'How would you like that?' As

Kate observed him in surprise he explained, 'The fishing rights go with the piece of land I've bought.'

'Oh! I say!' she teased. 'And I suppose you will have a boat moored at the bottom of your garden.'

'I might, but it won't be until I'm living there, and given the speed the builder is moving at it could be quite some time before I'm in residence.'

Alex had been listening wide-eyed to what they were saying and now he was finding his voice. 'So we can fish in the river!' he cried.

'You'd like that, would you?' Kate said, putting juice and cereal in front of him.

'You bet I would!' he whooped. 'Wait till I tell Dad.' And the two doctors smiled their relief above his small dark head.

When they rang Tom he was feeling weak after surgery and badly in need of something to raise his spirits. Alex's voice coming over the line, full of excitement at the things he was going to do with Daniel and Kate, was just what he needed to hear. If his boy was happy, then so was he, and when it was Daniel's turn to have a word he asked who Kate was. Was she a girlfriend?

'No,' he replied promptly. 'Kate is the daughter of the lady I'm lodging with and she's lovely with Alex. You need have no worries about him while she's around. She'll make a great mother one day, and now I'm afraid I'll have to go—the practice calls. Alex is going to be fine. Don't worry about him. Put yourself first for once.'

CHAPTER FOUR

'KATE BARRINGTON and Dr Dreyfus!' the headmaster of the village school exclaimed when they were shown into his office. He came out from behind his desk to shake hands with them and said, 'This is a pleasant surprise, if I may say so. It seems a long time since I last saw you, Kate, and who is this young man that you have brought to see me?'

Graham Henshaw had been headmaster when Kate had been Alex's age and for a good few years before that. He was a jovial man in his late fifties with a pleasant wife and two sons at university. The small school always came high in the league for excellence and it was mainly due to the hard work and dedication of its headmaster.

'His name is Alex,' Daniel told him, looking down at his young charge's dark locks. 'Last night I had to uproot him from Gloucestershire, where he lives, because of an emergency in his home life and bring him here, far from all the things that he is familiar with.

'We aren't sure how long Alex will be staying with us, but we know that it is important that he doesn't miss any of his schooling and have come to ask if you will take him as a pupil here until his home circumstances change.'

'And they are?' the headmaster questioned.

'Alex's father is bringing him up alone. Yesterday he had a serious accident while at work, which could keep him hospitalised for some weeks. He has asked if I will look after Alex until he is mobile again so he is staying with Kate and I at Jasmine Cottage.' Daniel smiled across at his companion. 'Kate has kindly offered to help.'

'I see,' Graham said with a smile of his own for the small boy standing uncertainly beside them. 'I'm sure that we'll be able to find you a place in our school, Alex.' He turned to Daniel and Kate. 'Any intake of new pupils has to be authorised by the Local Education Authority, who has to agree to accept them into the system by including them on their roll. I'll get on to them and ask that they put it through as fast as possible. There should be no problem when I explain the circumstances.

'In the meantime, bring Alex in to school. He can sit and watch and get to know the other children until I hear from the powers that be. You have the practice to consider, haven't you?'

Daniel nodded. 'Yes, and Kate is joining us there as soon as Alex is at school.'

'Really!' Graham exclaimed. 'That's great news. So where does Ruth come in all of this?'

'My mother is at my grandma's,' Kate told him. 'She has heart problems so Mum is looking after her and could be there for quite some time.'

'So you are both in the thick of it,' he said sympathetically, and Kate thought that she couldn't argue about that, with a broken engagement dying in the charity shop window and the man beside her still mourning the love of his life. But at that moment the needs of a small boy came before any problems that might exist in her own and Daniel's lives.

Boys of a similar age to Alex were playing football on a sports field at the side of the school building when they left, and he perked up when he saw them.

It must have reminded him of the other thing that had caught his interest and he said, 'When are you going to show me where the river is, Kate?'

'Now, if you like,' she suggested. 'Daniel has to go back to his patients but you and I have got all afternoon to wander around.'

'Take Alex to the place where we'll be fishing,' he suggested.

'Which is where?'

'You can't miss the building site. Look for a half-finished house. Every time I urge the builder to press on he reminds me that summer is past and days are short and nights are long. I'd been hoping to be in for Christmas, but there's no chance of that.'

She didn't want to think of Christmas, Kate thought. The longer it was in coming, the better. She was not going to be the life and soul of any parties this year, with the feeling of betrayed trust so strong within her. But if it should turn out that Alex was still with them then, she would have to make an effort for his sake.

After they'd said goodbye to Daniel they began to walk the short distance to the river, and as Alex took in all the new sights and sounds around him she thought wistfully that she wanted children of her own one day, and Daniel's obvious affection for the child at her side showed that he must have felt the same way once.

But now the hand of circumstance had put that pleasure

on hold for both of them. In her case a broken engagement, and in his something much worse.

When they came to the plot that he'd described, her eyes widened. Daniel was having his house built on the part of the riverside that had been her favourite place when she'd been young.

She and her friends had played on the grassy slope that would be his front lawn, and on the opposite bank was a park where they'd often seen the bright flash of kingfishers beside a lily pond.

There were men working on the house and as they observed them questioningly Kate told them, 'I've brought Alex to see the river. Dr Dreyfus said it was all right for us to come onto the site.'

The one nearest to them smiled and said. 'What he says goes. The doc's the boss, but I think we'd better find you both hard hats if we've got one small enough for your lad.'

'I've got one that my youngster wears when he calls on his way home from school sometimes,' one of the other men told her. 'He's about the same age as yours.'

'Does he go to the village school?' Kate asked.

'Er…yes,' he said, somewhat taken aback. 'Why do you want to know?'

'It's just that Alex is new around here and at the moment doesn't know any other children. He'll be going there on Monday for a visit, that's all, with a view to becoming a pupil.'

'Ah, I see,' he said as light dawned. 'Well, my kid's name is Scott Thompson. He's a good lad. I'll tell him to look out for your Alex, then.'

When they'd been kitted out with the hard hats they strolled past the workmen and went to stand where the river was skipping along frothily over a stony bed. Almost as if on cue, as Alex gazed at the water wide-eyed, a big silver fish swam past, swerving and diving with a sense of purpose that only it understood.

'What was it?' he cried excitedly as it disappeared from view.

'A salmon, I think,' she told him, pleased to see him enjoying himself.

They dawdled by the river until the light began to go. The workmen had already gone, and Kate decided that the least said to Daniel about that the better.

As they took the hats off and wrapped them in some plastic that was lying around she was taking note of the structure, and thought that the property when it was finished was going to be quite something. How often had Daniel wished that Lucy might have been spared to share it with him? she wondered.

It was easy to tell how much she'd meant to him, and she wished there was some way to break down the barriers he'd erected to save himself further hurt. Because she knew that was from where the reserve in him came. The wariness that she sensed whenever he thought they were getting too close. Didn't he realise that if Lucy had loved him as much as he'd loved her, she wouldn't want him to be alone for the rest of his life?

But she was the last person to be deciding what Daniel should, and shouldn't do in his private life when her own was in such a mess, and the memory of the wedding dress in the charity shop window came back to haunt her.

They all had their problems. Herself with no clear way ahead. Daniel denying himself the pleasures of family life. Her gran trying to get back to health and strength with a failing heart, and her mother cheerful as always, but far from home in a stressful situation.

Then there was Tom facing an uncertain future due to the seriousness of his injuries, and Alex, young and defenceless, who had been plucked out of the only security he'd ever known and brought to live in a strange place.

Out of all of them he was the one she was concerned for most and, taking his hand in hers, she said, 'Let's go and find Daniel, shall we, and tell him that we saw a salmon?'

They had to pass the school on their way to seek him out and, pointing to the single-storey building nearby that housed the doctors, Kate said, 'That is the surgery where Daniel and I will be working. When school is over one of us will come for you and take you there until we've finished for the day. You can take some of your toys there so that you'll have something to play with while you're waiting. Would you like that?'

He nodded, and she thought thankfully that Alex seemed contented enough in the circumstances, until he said in the next breath, 'Is my dad going to die?'

When Kate looked up Daniel was standing in the entrance to the surgery. He must have seen them pass the window and had come out to greet them, and she could tell by his expression that he'd heard what Alex had said.

'No. He's not going to die, Alex,' he said gently as Kate felt tears prick. 'It might be hard for him to walk for a while because it was a very nasty accident that he had, but do you know what? Your dad will get better a lot sooner if he knows that you are all right, and you *are* all right here with us, aren't you?'

Alex nodded. 'Mmm. I like it here.'

'That's good, then,' Daniel told him. 'Because we like having you here, don't we, Kate?'

'Yes, we do,' she agreed, glad to see Alex looking happy again.

'Do you want to come in and wait?' Daniel said. 'I've a couple more patients to see, then I'm finished for the day.'

When they went inside, Jenny on reception told him that his next patient had cancelled so there was no rush. She had a smile for Alex and when Daniel explained that he was staying with them and would be coming to the surgery after school each day, she said brightly, 'Well, this is a surprise!' She turned to Alex. 'Do you want to be a doctor, too?'

He was looking around him curiously. 'I don't think so,' he told her, and with his visit to the building site fresh in his mind, 'I'd rather be a builder in a yellow hat.'

'The men lent us hard hats,' Kate explained.

'Ah! So that's what you've been up to,' Daniel said laughingly. 'I hope you laid a few bricks for me while you were there as time is pressing.'

'Why is that?' she questioned.

'Why do you think?' he said wryly as they went into his consulting room. Jenny had taken Alex into the surgery kitchen for a drink and a biscuit and they were alone for the moment. 'The sooner my house is finished, the sooner Alex and I can move out of Jasmine Cottage and give you some breathing space.'

That hurt. Didn't he realise that she wanted to help with Alex? Give him some happy home life while his father was in hospital?

He'd seen her expression and said, 'Don't be upset,

Kate. I just want to do the right thing. You're lovely with Alex. Having lost both his mother and his sister, the boy is short of a woman in his life, and that is no criticism of Tom. He's doing a great job.'

'So is your eagerness to move into your own place your way of saying that if Alex is short of a woman's love, *you aren't?*' she interrupted coolly.

He was growing accustomed to her face, he thought, the spiky blonde mop, the coltish slenderness of her and most of all the warmth of her personality. He'd only known her for a short time yet she'd captured his imagination as no other woman had since Lucy had been taken from him.

He would have been lost without her the night before when he'd brought Alex to stay with them, and the more he saw of Kate the more he found that his determination to stay clear of relationships was weakening.

'No. It isn't. Just the opposite,' he said quietly. 'It might have been a short time ago, but not now. The way the three of us have been thrown together reminds me of my own happy family life when I was a kid and I can see what I'm missing. I've made my choice, as you know, and I never thought I would question it, yet I am.

'I said what I did about moving out as soon as possible because I can't help feeling that I've butted into your life at a time when you would rather have been alone, and now that Alex is here there are two of us presuming upon your good nature.'

'That isn't how I see it,' she protested. 'It was the other way round. I was the one who butted into your life, whether you wanted it or not, and you've helped me to climb out of a black pit of rejection. Given me the strength to bounce back after what Craig did to me, and when I think that tomorrow I'll be here, working in the practice as a GP, I am truly grateful for all that you've done for me. You even saved me the anguish of taking my wedding dress to the charity shop. Though I would never have let you do that in a thousand years if I'd known about Lucy.'

'All right,' he said with a smile. 'After that vote of confidence I'd hate to blot my copybook. The last thing I intended was to upset you. If you will put up with us, we'd love to stay for as long as it takes.'

At that moment Alex reappeared and Daniel said, 'My last patient of the day is in the waiting room, Kate. Do you want to wait for me or go on ahead?'

'We'll go home,' she said as it began to register that it was only since Alex had appeared on the scene that Daniel had begun to question his single status. Perhaps he viewed her role as the third member of the trio as coincidental, rather than meant to be.

Yet, whatever the circumstances, she knew one thing. Getting to know him had shown her what a real man was like. Where Craig had been unfaithful, Daniel was ever faithful and she had to admire him for it, even though she didn't entirely agree with his reasoning.

It appeared that Alex's arrival on the scene had caused him to have a rethink, but there was nothing to say that it wasn't just a spur-of-the-moment thing and that he would soon be back to his original resolve. If she was crazy enough to let herself fall in love with him, the hurt it could bring would make her broken engagement seem like a minor upset.

The patient that Daniel had referred to was Keith Baxter, who lived on a narrowboat moored in a nearby basin on the canal that ran parallel with the river. Until recently he had owned one of the cottages in the main street of the village, but the pull of the waterways had got to him and he'd sold his house and bought the boat.

Daniel had thought of doing something similar himself when he'd had nowhere to live while his house was being built, but Ruth's kind offer had been tempting and he'd put the idea out of his mind.

Yet he was always interested to hear what Keith had to tell him about life on the water and the social activities at the moorings where he was based. Though today it wasn't his beloved boat that Keith wanted to talk about. He had a health problem.

His skin had a yellow tinge to it as if he was slightly jaundiced and he explained that he'd just got over a gastric upset and was now feeling unwell with other discomforts.

'I've been binge eating, then feeling nauseous and bringing the food back,' he said. 'I just don't feel right somehow, and when I saw that I was yellow I thought I'd better get it sorted.

'It's a strange thing,' he went on to say, 'but my family are prone to this sort of thing. I can remember my father being like this when he was alive and he never knew what caused it.'

'It's possible that you are suffering from Gilbert's syndrome,' Daniel told him after he'd examined him. 'A mild liver infection that usually flares up after something else. In your case most likely the gastric upset, and it is hereditary. So if you ever have any children it is something that they might inherit too just as your father could have passed it on to you.'

'Ugh!' Keith groaned. 'That's great!'

'There's no need to get too upset,' Daniel explained. 'The good news is that Gilbert's syndrome is quite common and usually clears up of its own accord. But having said that, I'm going to send you along to the nurse for a blood test just to make sure that is all it is. The result should be back within three to four days so make another appointment to see me then on your way out.'

'Thanks, Daniel,' Keith said, getting to his feet and now bringing up the subject closest to his heart. 'When are you going to come and see the boat? You're welcome to bring Kate—that was Kate Barrington I saw talking to Jenny, wasn't it? I didn't know she was back in circulation, although maybe she isn't. She had a child with her.'

'I'm staying at the Barringtons' until my house is ready,' Daniel said abruptly, 'and the young boy that you saw is the son of a friend of mine who is in hospital. Kate and I are looking after him, so socialising isn't possible at the moment, I'm afraid.'

'Not a problem,' Keith said breezily. 'I'm sure I'll catch up with her soon. I'll see you around, Daniel.'

Not if I see you first, Daniel thought, nettled at the thought of Keith being interested in Kate. He liked the other man, but he had a reputation for being a womaniser.

He knew that his annoyance was due partly to the realisation that having Kate in his life was providing tantalising glimpses of what he was missing. But in his life she was, and the only way he was going to be able to resist her was by playing it cool for the time being, which was not going to be easy while they were living in the same house, working in the same practice and looking after Alex together.

Yet he was going to try. He had been too long on the path that he had set for himself when Lucy had died to abandon it so suddenly, and once Alex was asleep that evening he said, 'I'm going to turn in, Kate. I want to catch up on some sleep after being awake most of last night listening for Alex. I don't think we'll hear much from him tonight. He seems to be taking everything in his stride so far.'

'Like he was when he spoke to his father this morning?'

'Yes, Alex was fine, but Tom wasn't. He'd come round from surgery and was in the high-dependency unit in a lot of pain. We spoke to a nurse first and she said to keep the call short, so I let Alex do most of the talking. Hopefully by tomorrow they will have been moved him into an or- thopaedic ward.'

'Are *you* all right?' she questioned. 'You've been very quiet since we came home.'

'Yes. I'm fine,' he replied. 'I just have a lot on my mind. Such as what will happen to Tom and Alex if he can't ever work again. Then there is the matter of keeping an eye on the builders, and last, but by no means least, making sure that the practice runs smoothly.'

He wasn't going to tell her that the main thing on his mind was the effect that she was having on him. She was only just coming to terms with a broken engagement, and if she found out that he was lusting after her, the high opinion she had of him would topple off its perch in no time at all.

'Cross your bridges when you get to them,' she advised. 'It's early days to be worrying about Tom's future, and however long you have to wait for your house to be finished, in the end you will have a beautiful home. As for the practice, from tomorrow there will be three of us to carry the load. I met Miriam who was about to make a quick departure while I was at the surgery this afternoon, and she said she was pleased to hear that I'll be on the job tomorrow.'

'Good,' he said absently. He looked around the kitchen at the clutter from the evening meal. 'Leave everything. I'll clear away in the morning. Goodnight, Kate.'

When he'd gone she sat with elbows on the table and chin in cupped hands. There was something eating at Daniel that he wasn't prepared to discuss, she thought. But what was new about that?

The things he'd mentioned were responsibilities, but from what she'd seen of him so far he dealt with those sort of problems with a cool efficiency. The only thing that seemed out of character was the way he had chosen such a monastic way of life.

He didn't give the impression of being a defeatist, which only went to show how deep his hurt went, and now he had a constant reminder of it in the presence of the young brother of the woman he'd loved. Yet he hadn't hesitated for a second when Tom had made his frantic request.

She got to her feet slowly and, ignoring his instructions, began to tidy up the kitchen. There was no way that Daniel was going to have that chore facing him in the morning. If she couldn't compete with the woman he'd loved, at least she could try to make his life as stress-free as possible.

She became still, hands resting in warm suds in the sink as the realisation of what she was thinking registered.

She'd just admitted to herself that she wanted the love that Daniel wasn't prepared to give.

When the phone rang in the quiet house some time later it was her mother, wanting to know if everything was all right. They hadn't spoken the night before, so as yet she wasn't aware of Alex's arrival.

When Kate explained the circumstances Ruth exclaimed, 'The poor lamb! Look after him, Kate. He couldn't be in better hands than yours and Daniel's. How *is* my lovely lodger?'

'He's fine. We're a team, he and I. At least, that's what I think. I'm not sure what Daniel thinks, but he has made me see just how shallow Craig was.'

She couldn't see her mother's satisfied smile, but her approval came through in her voice as she told her, 'So keep up the good work.'

When Kate asked after her grandma her mother's voice still had a lift to it as she said, 'Gran is much better. The hospital is talking about a pacemaker in the very near future.'

As they were on the point of saying goodbye Ruth asked, 'What have you done with your wedding dress, Kate? It must be a painful reminder.'

'It's gone to the charity shop.'

'Oh! Taking it there must have hurt.'

'Daniel took it for me.'

'Really! How did that come about?'

'He offered. Although he wasn't sure if it was a good idea, me being in such a hurry, but I wanted it gone.'

'Yes. I can understand that,' Ruth said gravely.' But, Kate, sometimes these things happen for a purpose. The fates might have something better in store for you.'

'I hope so,' she replied, glancing upwards. 'But at the moment I very much doubt it.'

The following morning Kate told Daniel, 'One of the workmen at your site has a boy the same age as Alex. His name is Scott Thompson. It was his hard hat that his father lent us. Do you know anything about the family?'

'No, not really, but I know the guy you mean and he seems a decent sort. Yet I think that we should let Alex choose his own friends. He's a sensible kid, and now that Graham knows his home circumstances he'll keep an eye on him for us. I suggest that we both take him as it's his first day, and after that we drop him off on our way to the surgery each morning, and then one of us collects him when school finishes in the afternoon.

'Really, he's old enough to make his own way to us at the end of each day. We're only talking about a couple of hundred yards, but it's getting dark by the middle of the afternoon at this time of year and I'm not taking any chances.

'Tom has placed Alex in my care and I want to hand him back to him safe and sound when the time comes.'

'He certainly chose the right person when he asked you to look after his son,' she commented.

'He chose the *only* person,' he said whimsically. 'There wasn't anyone else to ask, and as for my side of it, Lucy asked me to look out for her dad and Alex. I said I would, and when I make a promise I keep it.'

'I can tell that,' she said wistfully.

'I wasn't making comparisons,' he explained quickly, observing the soft droop of her mouth. He'd just been stating a fact, not intending to remind Kate of the Craig fellow.

Daniel had no idea that Kate's moment of melancholy had nothing to do with her ex-fiancé. She was remembering another promise he'd made and on that occasion it had been to himself.

They'd seen Alex safely into school without any obvious reluctance on his part and when a smiling teacher had taken him in hand the two doctors made their way to the surgery.

As they got out of the car Kate was aware that Daniel was distancing himself from her now that Alex wasn't around. He'd shown a united front while the three of them had been together, but now it had disappeared. Although he did ask, 'Are you nervous at the thought of your first day back as a GP?'

'No. Not at all,' she said, stung into nonchalance. 'When one has worked in A and E, every other aspect of health care seems less challenging.'

'Such confidence!' he exclaimed with a grin. 'I'll watch your performance with interest.'

She had regretted her attitude almost before the words had come out and now Daniel had retaliated with smiling sarcasm.

'What's wrong?' she asked in a low voice. 'I thought we had become friends. Why are you being so aloof now that we're alone?'

'We *are* friends,' he said evenly. 'Don't ever have any doubts about that. We only met a short time ago, yet I feel as if I've known you for ever. You are the easiest of people to get to know.'

'So what's the problem?'

'That. That is the problem,' he said in the same level

tones. 'And now shall we get the day under way before Miriam sends out a search party?'

There wasn't a lot she could say to that so she followed him in, and as she was introduced to the staff and shown the room that was going to be hers, Kate began to unwind.

By the time she'd hung up her long winter coat and arranged the swivel chair behind the desk to her satisfaction he was observing her from the doorway and asking, 'Are you all right?'

'Er...yes,' she told him. 'The room is fine. The staff have made me feel very welcome and...'

He was shaking his head. 'I meant are you all right after our earlier moment of noncommunication?'

'Yes,' she said softly, 'and you know I do understand. What happened to you was awful, and how you choose to live your life is your affair and no one else's.'

'I'm relieved that you see it my way,' he told her, and wondered why he didn't sound more positive.

CHAPTER FIVE

KATE's first patient in her new role as a GP was a man with a streaming nose and hacking cough that she suspected might be allergy related as they had only surfaced since his wife had brought home a large, exotic, flowering plant from a recent shopping trip.

'She is insisting that it can't be the plant,' William Harris croaked, 'but I'm sure that it is. I was fine until she brought the ghastly triffid into the house.'

Kate sounded his chest and it was clear. So the cough did seem to be from some sort of irritation rather than a bronchial ailment.

'I'm going to prescribe you some antihistamines, William,' she told him. 'If it is an allergic reaction they should help to counteract its effect, and in the meantime see if you can persuade your wife to put the plant somewhere not so prominent for a while. You'll be able to tell whether it's causing your symptoms when you aren't near it for a few days.'

William Harris was followed by Katherine Donald, a young mother with her two-year-old daughter. Little Kirstie had swallowed a small plastic bead. 'I have to watch Kirstie all the time for this sort of thing,' Katherine said anxiously, 'but on this occasion I wasn't quick enough.'

'Has she got all her milk teeth?' Kate asked.

'No. There are two to come through and it is always the same when she's teething—everything goes into her mouth.'

'That's not uncommon, and the bead should pass through her in the normal way,' Kate explained reassuringly. 'Let me know if you have any concerns or worries but she'll be fine.'

And so it went on until Jenny brought her a coffee in the middle of the morning. When the receptionist had gone, Daniel appeared briefly to inform her that he'd phoned the headmaster to ask if Alex was all right and had been told that he was fine. That the first lesson had been art and he'd done a drawing that was quite exceptional for his age

'Were you aware of his artistic talent?' Graham had asked, and he'd had to admit that he hadn't been. Yet he hadn't been surprised as Lucy had been a talented artist herself.

'So Graham didn't think you were fussing,' Kate said.

'I don't know. He might have done, but I won't lose any sleep over it if he did,' was the reply. 'Alex's welfare is more important than what the headmaster thinks of me.'

She sighed and he observed her questioningly.

'What?'

'You would make a wonderful father.'

'And you a fantastic mother,' he said quietly, 'but for now let's make the most of being parents by proxy for Alex, shall we?'

'Yes, why not?' she agreed, thinking, What a state of affairs. They were both cut out for family life with parenting as a big part of it, but Daniel had just hit the nail on the head. Neither of them were moving in that direction at the present time.

'And now let's talk about your morning so far. How's it gone?' he asked.

That brought a smile. 'Great! I love it,' she told him. 'I've seen quite a few strange faces.'

'According to Jenny, that's about to change. She tells me that your next patient is known to everyone. Though I've had no cause to get to know him since I've been living in this rural paradise.'

'Who is it?'

'The arm of the law. Jim McIntyre, our local policeman.'

She smiled. 'Yes. I know Jim. He lives in a cottage beside the locks on the way to the canal basin. It's a beautiful part of the village and very popular with visitors. Do you know where I mean?'

'Yes. Keith Baxter, who came to consult me yesterday, has a narrowboat on the moorings up there. I almost thought of doing the same until I saw the land for sale beside the river. When he was here he caught sight of you and spoke as if he knew you.'

'I know who you mean. I've seen him around the village when I've been home on previous occasions, but I don't know him apart from that.'

Good, Daniel thought as the irritation that Keith had aroused in him the previous day diminished. Kate was too special for the likes of him. 'The policeman will be your last patient from the morning surgery and then it's home visits,' he said, getting back to the business of the day. 'And as you know the village and the surrounding area far better than I do, I'll leave you to it. Miriam has already started hers.'

'When are you going to take me to see Billy, the little lad with Sydenham's chorea?' she asked.

'So you haven't forgotten?' he commented, pleased that she'd remembered.

'No, of course not.'

'Tomorrow maybe. I passed him over to the neurologist once I'd seen his hands. He followed it up with various tests of his own and now Billy is in his care. But I call regularly to make sure that the poor kid is still having bed rest and that his mother is making sure he gets the sedation that has been prescribed for him.'

About to go back to his own room, he paused in the doorway and said, 'I'll pick Alex up this afternoon.' Seeing Kate look at him disappointedly, he sighed comically. 'Yes, I am fussing. I admit it. You can have your turn tomorrow.'

That made her laugh. 'All right. So we take it in turns.'

Jim McIntyre was a big, bluff, Lancastrian from one of the mill towns, who had moved into the Cheshire constabulary some years ago and was happy to be spending the last few years of his working life amongst country folk. Even though he was prone to say that wickedness came from within, and some folk there were no more saintly than those in the towns.

When he saw Kate seated behind the desk he said, 'This is a nice surprise, Kate. Are you back to stay?'

Was she back to stay? she thought. Yes, she definitely was, and the reason was just a few feet away in the next room.

'Yes. I am, Jim,' she told him. 'So what can I do for you?'

'I've got the copper's curse, lass. Sore feet from years of being on them.'

'So let's have a look, shall we?' she said with a smile for the grizzled policeman.

When he'd taken his shoes and socks off she exclaimed, 'Oh, dear! Those bunions must be painful, and they're making your toes overlap. It isn't going to be just a case of corn plasters or toe protectors, Jim. You need to see someone in orthopaedics.'

He groaned. 'I was expecting you to say that. The missus will say I told you so when I tell her. She's been on at me for ages to do something about me feet.'

'Well, better late than never. I'm going to make you an appointment with an orthopaedic consultant and will give you a ring when I've got a date. You're never going to catch law breakers if you have to chase them on those feet.'

'Aye. I suppose you're right,' he agreed reluctantly, and went on his way not exactly rejoicing.

Alex came out of school with a smile on his face and carrying a large sheet of white paper. When he saw Daniel he held it out for him to see and said, 'Miss said that she wants to put it up on the wall when I've shown it to you and Kate.'

'I'm not surprised. That is very good indeed. How about we take it to show your dad on Saturday before the teacher puts it on the wall?' he suggested, as it became obvious that Alex's first glimpse of the joys of village life had stuck in his mind. It was a drawing of the river as it flowed past the building site, and swimming along in its waters was a big silver fish.

'Yes!' he cried. 'Dad is good at drawing too, and so was Lucy.'

It was Daniel's turn to smile. It was obviously a real family talent, and for once hearing Lucy's name didn't bring its usual ache.

'Where's Kate?' Alex wanted to know.

'At the surgery and longing to know what your first day in a new school has been like. We're going there now so you can tell her all about it before we start seeing our patients. Are you hungry?'

'Yes. I'm starving.'

'That's no problem. She got you something from the bakery at lunchtime.'

'Kate is looking after me like Lucy used to, isn't she?' Alex said. 'I'm going to pretend that she's my big sister.'

'Yes, why not?' Daniel said, taken aback.

When Lucy had come into the conversation again he'd taken it in his stride, and almost as if he was testing him Alex went on to say, 'She would be pleased that I'm happy here with you and Kate. Lucy never liked it if any of us were miserable, did she, Uncle Dan?'

Dark eyes were fixed on him, waiting for an answer, and Daniel said slowly, 'No, she didn't, Alex. Your big sister liked to see everyone happy.' Having got the reassurance he'd asked for, Alex went chasing on ahead, making sure that the stiff breeze that was blowing didn't harm his work of art.

Following at a slower pace, Daniel was thinking that there had been no guile in what the boy had said. It had been just general conversation about someone they'd both loved. But though Alex would not have been aware of it, his innocent description of Lucy had held a message that he, Daniel, had needed to be reminded of. She *would* want him to be happy, and keeping his private life empty of all the things that created contentment wasn't going to bring that about.

'So?' Kate said as soon as they came through the door, 'How was school, Alex?'

'All right,' he said, waving the drawing under her nose. Having been forewarned, she was ready with the praise it deserved. 'That is very good indeed! Isn't it, Daniel?'

'Yes,' he agreed. 'The three of us are going to take it to show Tom on Saturday.'

'Good thinking,' she said as Alex tucked into the jam doughnut that had been waiting for him on her desk, and Daniel thought that it might cheer Tom up to find that an attractive and caring woman was involving herself in his son's well-being.

'So how do you feel after your first day back?' he asked after they'd shut out the chilly night and were having coffee in the sitting room at the end of the meal while Alex played with his toys up above.

She smiled her brilliant smile. 'Wonderful. I'd forgotten just how rewarding general practice can be. One's patients aren't just ships that pass in the night on their way to the wards or Theatre, or having been diagnosed as not serious are sent home. They are part of our small community and when it comes to their health the village doctor shares their smiles and their tears.'

'We certainly think alike on that,' he said. 'I've been

happier since I came here than I'd been in a long time. For one thing I met your mother and will always remember how good she was to me before she was called away. I hope she'll be back soon.'

'I hope so too,' Kate told him, 'but she won't leave my gran until she's sure she can manage. It would be easier all round if she would come to live with us but she won't be persuaded, so Mum is stuck there for the time being, just as Tom is far away in hospital. He must be missing Alex a lot. How long do you think he will be in there?'

'I really don't know,' he said flatly, noting that he didn't have a mention in her concerns. Her mother, yes, Alex, absolutely, even Tom, whom she'd never met, was being considered. But he had only himself to blame for feeling on the outside. He'd made sure Kate knew that *his* life was sorted.

Thinking that his downbeat tone was due to the weight of his worries for Lucy's family, she went and perched beside him on the side of his chair and placed her arm lightly across his shoulders.

'I'm so sorry that you are having to cope with this anxiety over Tom and Alex,' she said consolingly. 'But I'm sure it will all come right in the end, Daniel.'

He could hardly take in what she was saying so aware was he of her nearness. Her perfume, light yet tantalising, was in his nostrils. He could feel her soft breath on his face, and the curve of her breast was touching his neck as she leaned against him.

He turned his head slowly and as their eyes met Kate saw that their thoughts were running along different channels.

'What?' she questioned, moving her arm from around his shoulders.

'This,' he replied, and reaching up he cupped her face in his hands and brought it level with his. Then he was kissing her, long and lingeringly on the mouth, and as she kissed him back it felt so right that it took her breath away.

But there were footsteps on the stairs and Alex's voice calling, 'Can we phone the hospital again, Uncle Dan? I want to tell my dad about my drawing.'

'Yes, of course,' he murmured, putting Kate away from him gently. And turning to the table beside him, he picked up the phone and dialled the hospital, while she went to stand by the window to regain her composure.

They'd tried to get through a few times already since arriving home but the lines had been busy, and now as he dialled the number, with Alex standing beside him expectantly and Kate keeping a low profile, Daniel was telling himself that he wasn't being fair to the generous, loving woman that he'd just been kissing like a starving man at a feast.

There was an answer at the other end of the line this time and, putting his own affairs to one side, he asked to be put through to whatever ward Tom had been placed in.

'How's my boy?' was the first thing the older man said.

'He's fine, Tom,' Daniel told him. 'Right here beside me and longing to hear your voice. But first before I put him on, how are you?'

'Average,' Tom replied with a dry laugh. 'They are controlling the pain up to a point, and I am about to be involved in some in-depth physiotherapy tomorrow. I shudder to think how long it will be before I'm really mobile again, but thanks to you and your friend, Kate, at least one burden has been lifted from me. I know that Alex is in good hands and I can cope with anything if he's all right.'

'Well, here he is,' Daniel said, 'and you'll be seeing him soon. We're bringing him to see you on Saturday.'

'Wonderful! That's wonderful!' Tom said, choking on the words. 'I can't wait.'

Alex went to sit on the bottom step of the stairs while he talked to his father and Daniel went to stand by Kate, but before he could speak she forestalled him by saying in a low voice, 'What is it with you, Daniel? Are you playing mind games with me or what?

'I've already had one unpleasant experience with a man who didn't know his own mind. Craig used me and I don't want that to happen again. Since I've met you I've realised what it's like to know a man who stands out from the rest in every way but one.'

'And that is?'

'You know what I'm talking about, so don't pretend. Please, don't use me, Daniel, because I'm here, and Lucy isn't, and don't use the love that you had for her as an escape from anything that might seem too much like commitment.'

He sighed. 'So that's how you see me, is it? I suppose it's what I deserve. It was just that when you sat on the arm of my chair and were so close, I couldn't resist you.'

'Is it because I'm like her?' she asked. 'That would be the last straw. To be used because I'm her lookalike.'

'No!' he said vehemently. 'You are nothing like Lucy The exact opposite, in fact. I'm not looking for a clone. Lucy was small, dainty, with brown hair and eyes, and was a very tranquil person.'

'So I'm large, clumsy, and boisterous, am I?'

He shook his head despairingly. 'Don't put words into my mouth, Kate.

'You have your own kind of magic. Have no doubts about that. You came into my orderly existence like a whirlwind even though you were far from well, and nothing has settled into place since. I'm sorry if I've upset you and promise that it won't happen again.'

She wanted it to happen again, she thought. Time and time again, because she had fallen in love with him, but not under these circumstances. What she'd felt for Craig was as nothing compared to this.

At that moment Alex joined them, having finished talking to his father, and to all appearances normal life resumed.

Later, when he was asleep and Kate had just come off the phone after a long chat with her mother, Daniel said levelly, 'Regarding the weekend, Kate, I've been thinking that it would give Alex and Tom more time together if we booked in overnight at a hotel somewhere near the hospital. That way we could drop Alex off at the hospital on Sunday morning before we come back, which would give Tom some time alone with him for a couple of hours. Then we can drive back here in the afternoon, which won't interfere with him going to bed early, ready for school the next morning.' He paused for a moment, then went on, 'On the other hand, if you have something already planned for Sunday and don't want our visit to Tom to take up the whole weekend, feel free to say so.'

It would have been a good moment to tell him that all she wanted from the coming weekend was to be near *him*, and to bring some happiness to Alex and his father.

But in view of what had gone on earlier it wasn't a good moment for any further displays of feeling, so she just said, 'I have nothing planned, Daniel. I think it's a great idea, and typical of your usual common sense and thoughtfulness.'

He gave her a quick sideways glance. Had the reference to 'common sense' been a reminder of his promise not to get amorous again? But the bright blue eyes looking into his were clear and guileless and he decided that it was too much to hope that Kate was as attracted to him as he was to her.

After looking up places to stay in the vicinity of the hospital, he made the necessary reservations for a one-night stay at a hotel that was highly recommended and reported back to her that he'd booked a twin-bedded room for himself and Alex and a single one for her, and had also arranged for them to dine there on Saturday night.

As they drove out of the village on the Saturday morning, with Alex chattering excitedly to Kate in the back seat of the car, Daniel was thinking that this was the nearest he was ever likely to get to a family outing, and it was a chastening thought.

He'd felt that the decisions he'd made that had come from his grief when he'd lost Lucy would be easy enough to keep, and they had been. Until Kate had arrived in his life and turned it upside down, and now he felt that he was coming out of darkness into light.

He knew what Tom would say if he knew what was in his mind. 'Don't make your love for my girl into a shrine, Daniel,' he'd once said.

'I won't,' he'd told him.

Yet he had, and now it was taking all his strength of will to keep to his resolves.

The two on the back seat weren't having any such dismal thoughts, he noticed. They were playing a board game that required a throw of the dice to be a six for the player to begin and Alex was laughing gleefully. He had gone almost round the board while Kate, who was pretending dismay, still hadn't shaken the required number.

His spirits lifted. Live for the moment just this once, he told himself.

Make the most of this time together and see if you are still so captivated by Kate at the end of it.

Daniel had been quiet at breakfast, Kate was thinking, and he hadn't said much since they'd set off. But was it surprising when the focal point of the weekend was a visit to Tom whose life had been changed so drastically since the accident?

Yet he was smiling when they stopped on the motorway for coffee and a soft drink for Alex, and she thought that when he was happy she was happy, and when he asked whimsically if she was sure that there *was* a six on the dice, she sparkled across at him.

When they arrived on the ward Tom had just come back from physiotherapy and was looking pale and drawn, but when he saw Alex his face lit up and Kate wanted to weep for the pain of the separation from his son that he was having to endure, as well as the pain from his injuries.

They'd brought the drawing and Alex was pushing it into his hand and perching on the side of the bed as if hospital visiting was the normal. When his father had duly admired it, Daniel introduced Kate to him, and as they shook hands it felt strange to Kate to be in the company of the pleasant, middle-aged man who was Lucy's father.

'It's grand to meet you,' he said warmly, and with an affectionate glance in Daniel's direction, 'I will owe you both a great debt of gratitude when all this is over. I can tell that Alex is happy just by looking at him. They've screwed me together with nuts and bolts and suchlike, and have warned me that it will be some time before I am really mobile, but I promise that the moment I know I can cope, I'll relieve you of the responsibility.'

'There's no rush as far as we are concerned, is there, Kate?' Daniel said.

'Have they given you any idea how long you might be here?'

He sighed. 'No. Not yet. But when they do I shall ask for a carer to come in each day until I've got my strength back.'

That would be a grim time for him and Alex, Kate was thinking, and she was already planning how they could sort out the sleeping arrangements for Tom to join them at Jasmine Cottage. If Daniel didn't mind moving into the smaller of the two guest rooms, Alex and his father could have his room, with Alex sleeping on the blow-up bed that they used for that kind of occasion.

They left father and son together for a while and went for a walk in the hospital grounds, and as a chill wind whipped the colour up in her cheeks, Kate said, 'Tom could come straight to us when he's discharged.'

'Are you saying what I think you're saying?' he asked in amazement.

'Yes. And before you bring the subject up, my mother

won't mind. She's a pushover when it comes to helping people.'

'So are you.'

'Maybe. But it's an idea, isn't it? We'll just have to play it as it comes and when the right moment presents itself, put the plan to Tom.'

'You really are quite something,' he said, shaking his head in wonder.

'You're quite something yourself,' she replied. 'It might have been a lot less painful for you if you'd separated yourself from Lucy's family after she died, instead of being constantly reminded of her in Tom and Alex.'

'Is that what you would have done in my place?' he asked evenly.

'No. I suppose not.'

'So there you have your answer. *And* I'd made a promise, don't forget.'

'Hmm…of course you had. Why don't you tell me to mind my own business?'

Daniel didn't reply. He was wishing that Kate would stop doing things that increased his awareness of her because that was what was happening. He'd been going through the motions of living and not expecting anything to change.

But meeting her was bringing him back into the real world, making him remember that with love there was a special kind of joy as well as pain, and as they went back into the warmth of the hospital building and sought out a snack bar for a quick sandwich, he thought back to when they'd first met, and how much their lives had changed since that first, rather prickly encounter.

As she sat facing him, warming her hands around a

steaming mug of hot chocolate, Kate would have been amazed if she'd known where his thoughts had just been, as the next thing he had to say was, 'What sort of a sandwich do you think Alex would like?'

'Ham or chicken, I would think,' she told him, and watched him make his purchase with the easy efficiency that he did most things.

No one observing him would have expected the smile of the tall, dark-haired man at the counter to belong to someone who had committed himself to the sad past, and who was now being gently coaxed out of his protective cocoon.

When they'd finished their drinks he said, 'Shall we make our way back to the ward? Tom looked washed out and we don't want to overtire him. There's always tomorrow for him to spend some more time with Alex.'

When Kate nodded and got to her feet he said, 'I could soon get a guilt complex about swallowing up your weekend like this. What would you have been doing if you hadn't come?'

She smiled across at him. 'Nothing. Your conscience can remain clear. I came because I wanted to and nothing has changed.'

He touched her cheek gently. 'Bless you for that. We've been short of a woman's touch in our lives, Alex, Tom and myself.' Me most of all, he thought, and if I'm ready to admit it, where do I go from here?

They left Tom at five o'clock. His evening meal was due and he looked very tired, but he was smiling as he waved them goodbye because he knew that he would see Alex again in the morning.

When they arrived at the hotel Kate and Alex stood to one side in the foyer while Daniel confirmed their reservations with the people on Reception and Alex said suddenly, 'I told Dad that I'm going to pretend that you're my big sister.'

'I see,' she said slowly, 'and what did he have to say?'

'He said that Lucy would like that.'

'Have you told Daniel?'

'Yes.'

'And what did *he* say?' she asked, swallowing hard as she thought that in all innocence Alex would have hit Daniel's sore spot. The man who was turning away from the hotel desk with their room keys in his hand wouldn't have said anything to upset Lucy's young brother, but he could have seen it as a possible source of more disruption of his life coming from her direction, even though she had known nothing about it.

'He said that it was all right,' Alex replied.

'Everything is in order,' Daniel announced. 'Once we've tidied ourselves up there is a table reserved for us in the dining room, and after we've eaten there's a games room downstairs that might appeal to Alex.'

Kate was smiling a strained sort of smile and he wondered why. They had been in tune from the moment of leaving the village that morning and it was a good feeling.

As they were about to separate on the corridor outside their rooms he said, 'Give us a knock when you're ready to go down, Kate.' And when she nodded without speaking, 'What's wrong?'

'Nothing. I'm fine,' she told him unconvincingly, and went in and closed the door. She was deeply touched that

Alex should want to pretend that she was his sister, and hoped that Daniel had meant it when he'd said that it was all right.

Tears had been pricking ever since he'd told her and she hadn't wanted to shed them in front of Daniel. He would want to know why she was weeping and then she might discover that he'd only said what he had for the boy's sake.

It was clear that those who had loved Lucy were never going to forget her and that was how it should be. But where Tom and Alex had accepted that she was gone, Daniel wasn't as ready to let go.

She could tell that he was attracted to her, but apart from just that one time, he had been steadfast and unchanging in the promises he'd made to himself.

As she showered and towelled herself dry before putting on the change of clothing that she'd brought with her, the evening ahead was beginning to feel like an ordeal to be faced, instead of something that she'd been looking forward to.

But no one would have believed she'd been having those sorts of thoughts as she and Daniel kept Alex entertained while they were waiting to be served in the dining room. Or afterwards when she and he played table tennis in the games room with Daniel looking on in amusement as she kept missing the ball on purpose.

'You should have children, lots of them,' he said laughingly as she scrabbled around under the table to get it after a wild serve.

'I intend to, circumstances permitting,' she told him from a squatting position.

'And what does that mean?'

'That it takes two to make a baby, and for me it would

have to be because we loved each other very much. But I'm not having much joy in finding someone who would love me as much as I loved them.'

'There's plenty of time,' he pointed out abruptly. 'Look at it from the point of view that you've been spared from making a big mistake. Another time you'll know what to look out for.' He glanced across at Alex who was playing skittles. 'I think that we should call it a day for Alex. He's been on the go since early this morning.'

She already knew what to look out for, she was thinking, and she'd found it. Why couldn't she have met him before she'd got involved with Craig? Yet would it have made any difference if she had? Daniel would still be looking backwards instead of moving on.

It must be a humbling experience to be loved like that, but did he have to sound so patronising? Or maybe he was just letting her know that she needn't expect him to be in the running.

'Don't patronise me, Daniel,' she said in a low voice.

'What? That's a ridiculous thing to say.'

'Well, I am ridiculous, aren't I?'

'Not to me.'

'To you more than anyone.'

He shook his head. 'To me you are kind, funny, delightful in every way. If I ever caused you hurt I would never forgive myself. I've been living the kind of life I chose for quite some time. It came out of grief and devastation. If I'm going to change, I need time. Can you understand that, Kate?'

'Yes, of course,' she said gently, after listening to his toneless description of how his hopes and dreams had been blown away.

As they went up in the lift he said, 'I'm not intending leaving Alex alone once he's asleep. I've brought a book with me and will pass the time with that if you want some space. I feel sometimes that we don't give you a moment to yourself. But promise me that you won't go into the bar alone, or leave the hotel without telling me.'

'I'm not proposing to do anything like that,' she said with calm dignity. 'I thought we were a threesome, but enjoy your book. I'll watch TV for a while and then have an early night.'

When they stopped outside the door of Daniel's room she bent and gave Alex a hug. 'Goodnight, you precious child,' she said gently, and kissed him on the cheek. 'Go fast asleep for Daniel, won't you? We're going to see your dad again in the morning, and you don't want to be falling asleep beside his bed.'

As he nodded obediently she turned to the man standing silently beside him and said in the same soft tone that belied the hurt in her eyes, 'Goodnight to you too, Daniel. Sleep well.'

Sleep well, he thought dismally as the door closed behind Alex and himself. *He was insane.* How was he going to be able to sleep at all after letting Kate think he'd rather read a book than be with her? Every second spent with her was delightful. Yet he'd still backed off at the thought of them being alone together when Alex was asleep. But why, when the more he was with Kate the more the pain of losing Lucy was becoming just a memory?

He groaned inwardly. Having crossed that barrier, there were others to contend with. He knew that Kate was drawn to him. The way she'd kissed him back the other night had told him that. But would she feel she could trust him with her heart, knowing his past? Was he the one she would want children with at some time in the future? He wouldn't be if he carried on the way he was doing, that was for sure.

CHAPTER SIX

WHEN Kate went into her own room she undressed slowly and lay on top of the bed covers, gazing blankly up at the ceiling, but as the warmth of the room began to wrap itself around her she found her eyelids drooping and thought that at this rate she was going to be asleep before Alex.

A couple of hours went by and it was the ringing of the phone beside the bed that brought her back to wakefulness.

'Kate?' Daniel's voice said in her ear.

'Yes, what is it?' she answered drowsily.

'You were asleep! I'm sorry to have disturbed you.'

She was raising herself up on to the pillows. Was there something wrong with Alex?

'Is it Alex?' she asked.

'No. He's fast asleep. I've just been onto room service and ordered hot chocolate for two in the hope that you might still be awake. Do you feel like joining me, or shall I leave you to go back to sleep?'

She was on her feet and reaching for the white towelling robe that the hotel provided for its guests. 'I'll be right with you,' she told him, and padded into the room next door.

Her cheeks were flushed from sleep, her eye make-up smudged, and as she closed the door behind her Kate gave a big yawn. When she saw Daniel smile, she glanced in the mirror and grimaced.

'I look a mess,' she moaned, and now he was laughing.

'You'll have to console yourself with the thought that beauty is in the eye of the beholder.'

'Oh, yes,' she agreed doubtfully, and moved across the room to look down at Alex, sleeping the sleep of the innocent in pyjamas with a superhero design on the front.

'Life is so uncomplicated at their age, isn't it?' she said softly.

He had come to stand beside her. 'It should be, but I'm not so sure in Alex's case. For one thing, I can't see Tom ever being able to work again. He will probably gain some degree of mobility eventually but it will take time, and even then just coping with the basics will be difficult.'

'What exactly happened to him?' she asked. 'I know he had a fall, but not how, or why.'

'He fell off scaffolding and landed with his full weight on his knees, causing multiple fractures. I just wish my house was finished so that I could bring him and Alex to the village to live. That way I would always be on hand if they needed me.'

'Yes, but I *have* offered you a solution with regard to the immediate future, haven't I?' she said, looking up at him with her smudged eyes. 'And if you are still concerned about what my mother will say, when we get back we'll ask her. Just in case we have to put plan Jasmine Cottage into action.'

They were almost touching in their borrowed dressing-gowns and Kate was wishing she didn't look such a sight as he said in a low voice, 'You are too kind to me.'

A knock on the door announcing room service interrupted them, and they went to sit on the sofa and composed themselves. When they'd drunk the hot chocolate Kate got up to go. 'I'll see you in the morning,' she told him softly.

He was smiling across at her. 'Don't go yet, Kate.'

Framed in the doorway, she became still. 'Make up your mind. A couple of hours ago you couldn't wait to get rid of me. Now you've invited me to join you and when I'm ready to leave, you don't want me to go. What is it with you, Daniel?'

The smile had gone. 'I'm sorry. Forget I said that, and for the record the last thing I fancied doing earlier was spending the evening reading a book when you were only yards away. But apart from the fact that I knew that neither of us would want Alex to wake up and find us in bed together, I didn't want to send out any false signals that I mightn't be able to live up to.'

'And so what has changed since then?'

'Nothing,' he said flatly. 'I asked you to come and join me because I wouldn't leave Alex in here on his own, and I wanted to see you one more time before the day was over.'

'And now that you've seen me?'

'I'll be able to do what you told me to do.'

'What was that?'

'Sleep well, and I hope you do too.'

I doubt it she thought as she shut the door quietly behind her and went back to her own room. The man she'd just left had said that he didn't want to send out any false signals. Had Daniel meant that he wouldn't want her to confuse desire with real love?

* * *

It was still daylight when they returned to the village the following afternoon after a more subdued journey than the one going and Daniel said, 'Do you mind if we stop off at the building site, Kate? Some of the men were going to work yesterday and I'm keen to see what progress they've made.'

'Yes. It's fine by me,' she told him.

'And me,' Alex chirped, suddenly coming to life.

He had shed a few tears when it had been time to leave his father, and as the two doctors had stood by helplessly Kate had vowed to herself that father and son were going to be reunited at the first opportunity at Jasmine Cottage if Tom would accept the offer.

Alex was perking up now. To him the building site meant the river, and on a grey Sunday afternoon in early November it was the only thing moving when they got there. Yet Daniel was nodding approvingly as he looked around him. Progress had been made over the weekend. His new home was really taking shape at last.

But after all the months of waiting there wasn't the same sort of excitement that he'd felt when he'd first started the project because once he'd moved into the house he wouldn't see as much of Kate. They would meet up at the surgery, of course, but she wouldn't be sitting across the table from him at breakfast or there last thing at night when they went to their separate rooms.

As he watched Alex eagerly pulling her towards the riverbank he thought that she wasn't showing much interest in his new property and decided it was because she knew that if Alex was still around he would be taking him with him when he moved in.

As he wandered around what he'd intended to be his

dream home, for once it wasn't Lucy that he was wishing could be there to share it with him. Kate's face kept getting in the way.

The winter dusk was wrapping itself around the building site as he joined them at the water's edge and when he asked, 'Have you seen any big fish today?' Alex shook his head.

'Tell Daniel what we *have* just seen,' Kate said.

'A water vole,' he said excitedly. 'It looked like Ratty in *The Wind In The Willows*.'

'Really!' Daniel exclaimed. 'Where was it?'

'On the other bank,' Kate told him. 'I've just been telling Alex that Ratty might have been a water vole. They are very like a rat, but have a more bushy tail.'

He smiled. 'So speaks the country woman.'

'This part of the riverbank was our favourite place for my friends and I when we were kids,' she told him. 'I never thought then that I would one day meet the man who was going to build a house here.'

As they walked back to the car Daniel said, 'Is that why you have nothing to say about my future home, because I'm trespassing on your memories?'

'No! Of course not,' she protested, knowing that if she wanted to keep it light she couldn't tell him that she wanted to live there with him in what to her was the village's heartland. But with Lucy's ghost ever present, as far as Daniel was concerned, she knew it was an impossible dream.

Monday morning at the practice brought the usual ills for the time of year in the form of coughs and colds, with the occasional patient suffering from a more serious complaint. Frances Tennant, a friend of Kate's mother, unfortunately seemed to have fallen into the latter category. She was normally a very active member of the community. A force to be reckoned with in the Women's Institute. A leading light in church activities. Responsible for fresh flowers in the church on Sundays and the distribution of them to the sick afterwards. Plus the organising of a yearly coach trip to the seaside. All functions that she performed with relish. But when Frances seated herself opposite her in the middle of the morning Kate saw immediately that her usual drive was missing.

'I've got a lump under my arm, Kate,' she said, 'and I don't feel at all well. I'm tired all the time and, no matter how cold the night is, when I'm in bed I'm sweating a lot.'

When she removed her jumper Kate saw that there was indeed a swelling in one armpit.

'It could be something to do with your lymph nodes,' she told her, 'which would cause you to feel generally unwell. I'm going to arrange for you to have a biopsy taken from the tissue of the swelling and we'll take it from there. In the meantime, rest as much as you can, drink plenty of fluids, and the hospital will ring you as soon as they have an appointment date.'

Frances was looking more relaxed with the thought of prompt attention to her problem. Action was what the elderly human dynamo thrived on. There had to be no loose ends for the woman sitting opposite Kate, and in keeping with that she asked in what was more like her usual brisk tone, 'Are there any signs of your mother coming back yet?'

'Not at the moment,' Kate told her, 'though my gran is much improved.'

'Does she know that you and Dr Dreyfus are alone at

Jasmine Cottage? I would have thought he might have moved out when you came home to stay.'

Kate turned away to hide a smile. This was Frances in her role of busybody, she thought, and was tempted to tell her that if there was one man who wasn't going to take advantage of her it was Daniel, and that she almost wished he would.

Instead she said breezily, 'We aren't alone, Frances. We have an eight-year-old boy staying with us that we are looking after for a friend of Daniel's who is in hospital, and that gives us no time for anything other than playing the roles of landlady's daughter, paying guest and childminders.'

'Really!' the woman sitting opposite exclaimed. 'So there's a child in the house! I wasn't aware of that.'

'No? Well, now you are,' Kate said with a smile, thinking that was a first. Frances not knowing something that was going on in the village.

But when she'd gone, Kate was in a solemn mood. A couple of worrying illnesses had come to mind when she'd seen the swelling in Frances's armpit. Both connected with the lymph nodes, and both serious. Yet there was no point in speculating until the results of the biopsy were available.

It was the only drawback to rural health care, having to tell a patient who was either friend or acquaintance that they had a life-threatening illness. It was difficult enough passing on those sorts of tidings to a complete stranger, but twice as hard when one knew the person.

When it was time for house calls Daniel said, 'I'm going to see Billy, the boy with Sydenham's chorea. Do you want to come along?'

'Yes. I do,' she said immediately, and after a quick tea-break, they drove to the Gileses' property in its elevated position.

Going inside the cluttered, dilapidated house, Kate thought that where talking to Frances had been like dealing with the over-organised, this was an example of the opposite. Personally she preferred the happy medium.

Daniel was relieved to see there were no signs of the repetitive neck movements when he examined Billy, signifying an improvement, but the two doctors knew that it didn't mean they wouldn't come back.

'Our Billy's fed up of being in bed,' Linda Giles said. 'When can he get up?'

'When are you due to see the neurologist again?' Daniel asked.

'Next week in Outpatients.'

'Have you got transport?'

'No. Not really. All we have is the farm truck that his dad uses, and it's a smelly old thing.'

'I'll ask one of my staff to arrange an ambulance,' he told her. 'It's clear to see that Billy is much better, but these things can't be rushed. It isn't easy to tell if the improvement is the result of the mild sedation that the neurologist has put him on or the bed rest.'

He turned to Kate. 'If the illness had remained untreated the constant movement could have eventually affected his heart. Billy, could you hold out your hands like I showed you for the new doctor,' he said, and as Kate observed keenly it was there, the backward splaying of the fingers.

'Very interesting,' she commented thoughtfully as they drove away.

He nodded. 'The next time I call I'm going to mention

getting them rehoused by the council if Billy's parents will agree to it.'

'So who does the house belong to?' she'd asked. 'Very often it is rented from the farmer who employs the man.'

'Yes. That's how it is with them and you've seen what it's like. If the council would put them into one of their properties for health reasons it could only benefit them all.'

'Those children could do with better living conditions, that's for sure,' she agreed.

'I can't argue with that,' he told her, 'and as for young Billy, he is a very interesting case, don't you think?'

'Yes. I do. A lot of our patients have problems that give food for thought. But so far there are none as rare as his. I had a consultation this morning with someone who may have trouble ahead.'

'Who was it?'

'A friend of my mother's.'

'And what did you suspect?'

'Hodgkin's disease or some sort of leukaemia.'

'So you've arranged for a biopsy.'

'Yes. Frances is very involved in the life of the village and won't take it kindly if she's ill.'

'She'll only be like a lot more patients, then,' he said dryly. 'What is it with her? Does she think she's invincible?'

'Something like that. But she was in a chastened state this morning. Though not so much so that she didn't make known her feelings about you and I living on our own at Jasmine Cottage.'

'What?' he exclaimed angrily. 'The nerve of her!'

'Frances is like that. Don't let it get to you.'

He was not to be placated. 'And so what did you tell

her? That you are quite safe with me? That I am living a life of self-imposed celibacy?'

Kate frowned. 'No. I did not. I would never discuss you with anyone else, but if I had said that it would have been true, wouldn't it?'

It seemed that the discussion was at an end. 'I'll take you back to the surgery to pick up your car so that you can carry on with your own calls,' he said flatly.

'Fine,' she said coolly, taken aback that they were so suddenly out of tune, and after that there was silence in the car until Daniel dropped her off outside the practice and went on his way.

As she was about to transfer to her own car, Richard Thompson, the builder whose son had befriended Alex at school, came hobbling onto the forecourt and said, 'Could you spare me a minute, Doc? I've just wrenched my ankle, jumping down off a ladder on the site, and would be obliged if you would take a look at it. I don't think I've broken anything, but it's very painful.'

'Yes, of course,' she said. 'Come inside.' When he'd eased himself onto a chair in her consulting room, she said, 'OK, take off your boots and your sock.'

When he'd done as she asked Kate saw that the foot was already swelling and when she felt it gently he grimaced.

'I think it's a bad sprain,' she told him. 'Your foot would swell with a sprain just as much as with a fracture. We'll get the nurse to put a cold compress on it, or maybe witch hazel, and then go home and rest it for the remainder of the day. If it is no better tomorrow, I suggest that you go to A and E to have it X-rayed.'

As he put his footwear back on, Richard said, 'So how's the youngster settling in at school?'

'He seems fine,' she told him.

He nodded. 'My Scott's been getting on well with young Alex, and of course they're in the same class, which is nice. He tells me they have a kick-around with a ball in the schoolyard during the break.'

Kate smiled, 'Yes, and we're so pleased that Alex has made friends with your son. He talks about Scott quite a lot, so thanks ever so much for your help there.'

'Not at all,' he said, and on the point of hobbling off in search of the nurse he added, 'I hope that the doc hasn't seem me coming here. He's panting for us to get his house finished.'

'Yes, I know he is,' she told him, and thought that *she* wasn't.

Why had he been so tetchy with Kate? Daniel was thinking as he drove up to one of the hill farms where an elderly patient with arthritis would be looking forward to his visit.

Maybe it was the strain of trying to stay immune from her appeal that was getting to him. It was ridiculous to pretend that he wasn't affected by her. She was never out of his mind. When she was near he was so conscious of her presence he couldn't think straight. Kate was part of his life now. He couldn't imagine it without her.

But he'd carried his love for Lucy around with him for a long time. It had been like a protective shield against leaving himself open to a repeat of the pain he'd suffered when he'd lost her.

Last night in the hotel he had realised that the pain was gone, though the memory lived on, and now, when there was light in his darkness, he was still hesitating. Why was

it that everything else in his life was clear and uncomplicated except this? His commitment to Alex and Tom
caused him no grief. His career was fulfilling. The place
where he had chosen to live was delightful, and soon he
would have a beautiful house to live in.

Tom had warned him not to turn his love for Lucy into
a shrine, but he hadn't been able to stop himself, and that
situation could have gone on for ever if he hadn't met Kate
of the blithe spirit and loving heart who had already been
treated badly by another man. God forbid that he should
bring her more hurt.

Kate was still out seeing her patients when Daniel got
back, but Miriam had returned and he found her in her
room, having a quick lunch.

'How do you think the new arrangement is working,
Miriam?' he asked.

'Good,' she said with a smile. 'It goes without saying,
Daniel. Three doctors instead of two *and* our new member
is Kate Barrington. She was an asset when she was here
before and will prove to be the same again.' As he listened
in amazement to Miriam actually approving of something he'd done, she went on to say, 'I know I haven't
exactly been a ray of sunshine since you took over, but
I've got health problems of my own, and where it should
be a case of "physician, heal thyself" I've been too busy
with this place to get down to sorting them. But now that
is happening, thanks to you.'

'Are they anything I can help with?' he asked in immediate concern. 'I have been worried about you, you
know. But I didn't like to interfere in your private life.'

The smile was there again. 'Thanks, Daniel, but, no, I

can sort them myself, and if I find that I can't, I will ask your advice.'

'Sure,' he said easily, and went to have his own lunch, glad that at least Miriam was now happy and content.

As Kate had passed the charity shop window on her way to her first call of the day she'd seen that the wedding dress had gone and the gloom that had descended after leaving Daniel deepened.

Yet she told herself as she drove on that it was what she wanted, an end to her relationship with Craig, and now she'd got it. Who had bought the dress? she wondered, and hoped that she wasn't going to be present if the purchaser was planning on walking down the aisle of the village church in it.

It was almost as if the mischievous fates had tuned into her thoughts as when she arrived back at the surgery Jenny on Reception beckoned her over and said in a low voice, 'Our Sarah has made an appointment to see you this afternoon. She's not at all well and is getting married in three weeks' time.

'She's only eighteen and her dad and I think it's a bit young, but they're so much in love and have been going out together since they were at school, so we've given them our blessing. It won't be a big affair. Money is tight. But would you believe it? She's found herself a lovely wedding dress in the charity shop, of all places.'

She could believe it all right, Kate thought as the implications of what Jenny was saying sank in. She hoped they wouldn't invite her to the wedding. Dredging up a smile, she asked, 'So what date is the wedding and where is the ceremony taking place?'

'It's the last Saturday in November and she's getting married in the village church, of course. There will be just a few relatives there and the staff from the practice, as I look upon everyone here as my friends. You'll be getting an invitation shortly.'

Covering up her confused emotions with a bright smile, Kate went into her room and closed the door. The idea of seeing Sarah in what had been *her* wedding dress was extremely daunting, but she couldn't disappoint Jenny. However, there was also the fact that if Tom hadn't been discharged from hospital by then, they couldn't miss visiting him on the Saturday. Seeing Alex was the only thing keeping him sane in the present circumstances, and they couldn't deny him that. Maybe they could visit Tom on the Sunday.

Into the midst of the mental chaos that Jenny had created came Daniel to apologise, but when he saw her expression he halted in his tracks and said, 'Surely I'm not responsible for making you look like that.'

She shook her head. 'No. Jenny is the cause of it, I'm afraid.'

'Jenny? Why? What has she done?'

'Her daughter is getting married in three weeks and we are invited.'

'So what's wrong with that?'

'Nothing. Except that Sarah has bought my wedding dress.'

'Oh, dear!' There was concern in the dark hazel eyes looking into hers. 'Didn't I tell you that it was a crazy idea, sending it to that place so soon?'

'Yes, you did. I don't need reminding, though. And what about Tom? If he is still in hospital, we can't miss visiting him.'

'That can be sorted. But, Kate, the one person who matters most in this situation is you. We could make an excuse not to go, I suppose.'

'We can't do that to Jenny,' she said sombrely. 'She's known *me* since I was so high, and *you're* her employer. If we're invited, we should be there.'

'I came to apologise for what I said earlier,' he said wryly. 'But it would seem that since then you have had more to be unhappy about. Will you forgive me?'

She sighed. 'Yes, of course. Frances is enough to make anyone edgy, and with regard to the dress, it was all that young Sarah could afford, according to her mother, so at least I know it has been bought by someone who will be happy to wear it.'

He went across to where she was hunched in the chair behind the desk. Taking her hands in his, he raised her gently to her feet. As their glances met he said softly, 'You are as charitable as you are enchanting.' As his hold tightened. 'Don't ever change, Kate.'

A tap on the door broke into the special moment and Kate held back a sigh as one of the practice nurses appeared with a query about blood tests that Daniel had asked to be done for one of his patients. Leaving them to sort it out, she went to the bakery across the street for a sandwich and thought that it was turning out to be a strange day.

There'd been Frances who didn't know how to mind her own business. Then, still on the down side, the short, sharp, exchange of words with Daniel when unthinkingly she'd told him what Frances had said, followed by an uplift when Richard Thompson had provided the cheering news about Alex and his son.

But that had been followed by another downward curve when she'd seen that the wedding dress had gone from the window of the charity shop, and no sooner had it registered than Jenny had been there with the news that young Sarah was going to be married in it.

It was all very mind-blowing, but what stood out like a jewel in a crown were the tender moments she'd just spent with Daniel. Was he coming round to her way of thinking? she wondered. Or had it just been an emotional moment that he was now regretting?

CHAPTER SEVEN

WHEN she had spoken to her mother the night before, on their return from visiting Tom, Kate had asked her if she would mind if they brought him to Jasmine Cottage when he was discharged from hospital.

'Of course I don't mind,' Ruth had said. 'The poor man sounds as if he needs some tender loving care, and between us you and I can provide it. Also you know that I have a soft spot for my lodger and by helping Tom we will be taking some of the burden of care off Daniel. I have to hand it to him, taking responsibility for the family of that poor girl he was going to marry.'

'Don't mention that if you speak to him, will you?' Kate had said from the privacy of her bedroom. 'I'm not sure whether Daniel would want me to tell anyone about Lucy and, Mum, I'm not certain that Tom will agree to coming here to convalesce. According to Daniel, he's normally very independent, and is doing a good job of bringing Alex up on his own. The accident is something that came out of the blue and he must be devastated. Yet he won't want to be an object of pity.'

'So you'll have to persuade him,' she'd said calmly.

'I'm intending being home soon myself. Your gran is talking about going to live with Aunt Lydia, who is more of her generation than we are, and as you know the two sisters have always been close. So if that is what she decides to do, and I'm pretty sure it will be, I'll organise the move and see her settled at Lydia's, then I'll come home. It will be lovely having my daughter back in the nest, so I suppose I do have *something* to thank that wretched Craig for.'

'The way things are going, you might have a houseful,' Kate had reminded her.

'The more the merrier,' she'd said laughingly.

Kate had already told her mother about Daniel's tragic loss, one night when Ruth had said that she couldn't understand him not being in any kind of a relationship. When she'd heard what had happened she'd been appalled.

When they spoke tonight she knew her news would still be far from uplifting, but her mother would want to be told that Frances wasn't well. She would also ache for her daughter when she heard that Kate was going to have to watch Sarah standing at the altar in her wedding dress.

But life wasn't all dark and dismal, she thought as she went to meet Alex from school. He was happy in the strange new life they'd brought him to, and just a short time ago she and Daniel had been on the same wavelength. There was no telling what might have happened if they hadn't been interrupted.

Her blissful imaginings didn't last long. When they got back to the surgery Daniel had a smile for Alex and for her just a question along the lines of whether she knew that Sarah was coming to consult her later in the afternoon.

'Yes. Jenny mentioned it at the same time that she told me about the dress,' she replied.

'So how did it go today?' he asked Alex, who was tucking into the snack she'd provided.

'OK,' he replied. 'We had art again. Scott and I played football, too.'

'I was talking to Scott's dad today,' Kate commented. 'Richard Thompson was one of my patients.'

'I see. And what was wrong with my best joiner?' Daniel asked as she'd known he would.

'Just a sprained ankle, I think. He'd jumped down off a ladder and landed awkwardly. I sent him to the nurse to have a cold compress put on it and told him to go home afterwards and rest it. I suppose that will mean more delay on the house, won't it?'

Daniel frowned. 'And I suppose you think I would have preferred to have him hobbling around the site all day. Is that it?'

'I don't think anything of the kind,' she said in a low voice, making sure that Alex was watching television in the staffroom behind Reception and couldn't hear them. To avoid any further conflict, she went into her room and closed the door behind her.

It wasn't working, she thought miserably. She was prepared to take account of *his* feelings, but he wasn't making any allowances for *hers*.

But how was she going to stay away from Daniel? Living with him, working with him. It had been a mistake, falling under his spell like she had. She should have forgotten about working at the surgery and gone to live elsewhere the moment she'd known his heart belonged to someone else.

The village was her home, though, she thought rebelli-
ously. She was enjoying being back in general practice and
knew that her mother was pleased to have her home once
more. So she was staying put. Somehow she would cope.

'Hello, Sarah,' Kate said with a smile for the pale young
bride-to-be as she seated herself opposite. 'What can I
do for you?'

She'd been eleven years old when Sarah had been born
and had been forever round at Jenny's house, asking if she
could push the baby out, and now here she was, a pretty
young thing looking pale and apprehensive, all grown up
and about to be married.

'Whenever I have anything to eat, I bring it back up,
Kate,' she said, and asked hesitantly, 'Is it all right to call
you that, or should I call you Dr Barrington?'

'Kate will do fine,' she said easily. 'I've known you too
long for you to call me anything else. So what about this
vomiting, Sarah? Could you be pregnant.'

She shook her head and her long blonde hair swung
gently from side to side. 'No, I wanted to wait,' she said
as tears threatened. 'But now I'm scared that I'm going
to die because I can't stop being sick.'

'Do you get stomach pains or indigestion, or a nasty
taste in your mouth?' Kate asked.

'No. My stomach just goes all queasy and then I'm sick.'

'Are you worried about the wedding at all? That kind
of vomiting can sometimes be brought on by stress.'

'I'm not worried about the actual wedding. I've bought
a lovely dress from the charity shop, but Jason's parents
are upsetting me. They say they're not going to be there.
That he's too young for such responsibility.'

'And what does he say?'

'That he loves me and wants to marry me more than anything, but they won't change their minds and I can't stop worrying about it.'

'And it's affecting your stomach from the sound of it. A lot of people vomit under stress. It's one of the body's ways of reacting to it. But we'll have a scan done just to be on the safe side, and in the meantime don't let your future in-laws spoil your big day.' She patted Sarah's hand sympathetically. 'With regard to the vomiting, try having small snacks instead of big meals. You might find them easier to keep down, and, Sarah, you're going to make a lovely bride. Try to put all your worries to one side and be happy that Jason loves you so much.'

Sarah was smiling now. 'The wedding dress I've got is really lovely, Kate. I'm longing for Jason to see me in it.' Now there was wistfulness in her smile. 'I just wish that I could be the first one to wear it. I keep wondering where it came from and whose it was.'

'I can answer both of those questions for you,' Kate told her. 'It was mine, Sarah, and it has never been worn before. I was engaged but we called it off, and I was left with a wedding dress that I had no use for. So you *will* be the only bride to wear it, and I will be there to see you in it, wishing you every happiness.'

'And you won't mind?' she asked in tremulous amazement.

Kate sighed. 'To be honest, I thought I would, but I don't, not now. If it helps to make you happy then I'll be happy too. Do you think that where it has come from could be our little secret?'

'Yes,' Sarah said, brightening. 'And every time my insides start churning I'll go and look at our dress and know that everything is going to be all right.'

'It isn't *our* dress,' Kate told her gently. 'It's yours, Sarah, and you will be a lovely bride.'

For the rest of the afternoon she was kept busy with little time to dwell on anything other than the needs of those attending the surgery, and when it came time for her last appointment Jenny was there to remind her that it might drag on a bit because of the person wanting to consult her.

As she was about to call the patient in Daniel appeared and said, 'I see that you've got Ed Fellows to finish off the day. Alex and I will go on ahead and I'll get the meal started.'

'Yes, sure,' she agreed, and as the door closed behind him she thought that if it wasn't for Alex being used to having her around at his bedtime, she would go into the town, have a meal there and maybe go to the cinema to give Daniel and herself some space.

But routine was very important in Alex's life at present. It gave him a feeling of security that he needed badly, and there was no way she was going to do anything to unsettle him while he was so happy with them.

Ed Fellows was a farmer of fifty years plus and not much loved by members of the practice because he always had some sort of gripe when he came for a consultation, but today the wind was taken out of his sails when he saw Kate behind the desk.

'How long have you been back in the surgery, Kate?' he asked.

'Not long, Ed. But I'm here to stay this time,' she said with a smile, and thought that saying it out loud had a comforting feeling.

'I see. Nobody told *me* you were back,' he said grumpily.

The smile was still there. 'My return wasn't a major event, I'm afraid,' she told him, and wondered what he would say if she explained that it was the result of a broken engagement.

Instead she asked, 'So what can I do for you today?'

'You can check my blood pressure,' he said promptly. 'I've been having some nasty headaches over the past few days, and the last time I had anything like that I ended up in hospital because it was at a dangerous level. I've been on medication ever since and it's been spot on, but it doesn't feel like it now.'

'It's fine,' she told him when she'd done the test. 'The headaches might be due to stress or eye strain. Have you been getting overtired or overwrought?'

He sighed. 'I'm always tired and overwrought. The farmer's life is not a happy one these days and I soon get cantankerous because I've got a short fuse. We farmers have to work long hours to make a living and there are so many rules and regulations we have to adhere to. Elsa, the wife, wants me to sell up, but this place is in my blood. It's where I was born, and where I want to die…but not yet.'

'Absolutely,' she agreed. 'So we'll try something else. I'm going to examine your ears.'

When she'd done so she asked, 'Where are the headaches? Left side, right side, over the temples?'

'The pain is down the left side of my head.'

She nodded. 'I thought so. You have an infection in

your left ear. That will be the cause. I'm going to put you on a course of antibiotics. Make sure that you take them all, and if it hasn't cleared up by then, come back to see me.'

He was getting to his feet. 'Aye, all right, and thanks for putting my mind at rest. By the way, how's your mother?

'She's fine. Mum is at my grandma's at present. She hasn't been well and Mum is looking after her.' They chatted a few minutes more before he went ambling off, and she thought that it was a shame that the life he loved was proving so stressful.

As Daniel drove along the main street of the village with Alex beside him he saw that the small florist's shop where the young bride-to-be worked was still open, so he stopped the car and took his small passenger inside with him.

It was Sarah who came from the back of the shop to serve them and he said, 'I want some roses, please, Sarah.'

'For a blonde or a brunette, Dr Dreyfus?' she asked.

'Er, a blonde,' he replied, a little taken aback. 'Why do you ask?'

'I have this thing about roses. I always say to customers, red roses for a brunette and cream or apricot for a blonde.'

'So apricot and cream roses it is, then.'

'I'll soon be making a bouquet for myself,' she said shyly as she began to make an attractive arrangement of long-stemmed roses. 'Has Mum told you I'm getting married?'

'Yes, she has,' he replied, with the memory surfacing

of Kate's horror at the thought of seeing her wedding dress again…on someone else. 'Congratulations, Sarah.'

'I was at the surgery this afternoon and Kate and I had a lovely chat,' she informed him.

'About your wedding, I suppose.'

'Yes. That and other things.'

What other things? he wondered as he made a quick exit. He'd like to bet the wedding dress wasn't amongst them if it had anything to do with Kate.

When she arrived home he was in the kitchen, grilling slices of chicken breast, while vegetables simmered on the hob.

Alex was doing a drawing and when he saw her he said, 'You've got some flowers…' His voice trailed away and when she turned round Daniel was behind her with his finger to his lips.

'What is going on?' she asked.

He took her hand and led her into the dining room where the table was set for the meal, and beside her place were the roses. She walked across slowly and picked them up without speaking, then began to read the card that was with them.

It said, 'I've been a bore and a misery twice today and you don't deserve it.'

He watched as her colour rose. 'The flowers are beautiful,' she said. 'I'll go and get a vase.' And without further comment she left him standing there while she went to the pantry where her mother kept such things on the top shelf.

He watched in silence as she arranged the flowers, and with weddings very much on the agenda he had a vision of her walking towards him down the aisle of the village church in a dress of rustling ivory brocade and carrying cream roses.

In that moment he knew that was what he wanted. Kate in his life for ever. He stepped towards her, but there was no melting tenderness this time in the eyes meeting his, just a kind of wariness, and as that registered Alex called from the kitchen, 'Uncle Dan, the chicken is beginning to burn.'

He caught it just in time and as he drained the vegetables and served up the meal the moment of revelation was put on hold, and the opportunity to tell her how he felt didn't present itself again as once Alex was asleep Kate came downstairs dressed in a short black jacket and jeans and announced, 'I'm going to the pub.'

'Why?' he asked. It was the first time she'd been out on her own since Alex had come to stay.

'Do I have to give a reason?'

'Yes,' he replied doggedly.

'All right, then. I'm giving you some space. We are in each other's company too much. If it hadn't been for upsetting Alex, I would have eaten out tonight and then gone to the cinema.'

'I see, and would that have had anything to do with the kind of day you've had?'

'It might have, but it wasn't all upsetting. I had a chat with Sarah when she came to consult me and the subject of the wedding dress came up. I surprised myself by telling her it had been mine and that I was happy to know that she in particular would be wearing it.'

'You weren't happy this morning. What made you change your mind?'

'A few things. She's a sweet girl, and I'd forgotten how I used to push her out when she was a baby, and sometimes help to feed her. Suddenly it all fell into place as if it was meant, and when the day comes, I will be fine.

'The poor thing is a bag of nerves because the bridegroom's parents are objecting to the wedding. They think their son is too young, and because she's so stressed Sarah keeps vomiting. It sounds as if her stomach is having a reflex action every time she has something to eat, but I'm sending her for a scan to be on the safe side.'

'Thank goodness for that, then,' he said. 'Not because Sarah is having stress problems, but because *you* won't be hurting on the day of her wedding when you see her in your dress.'

'It's not my dress any more. It's hers, and I can't think of a better closure for my relationship with Craig than seeing her in it. I've been moving on almost from the moment I came home, but that will really be a fitting end to the whole sorry episode.'

She'd been holding the doorhandle all the time they'd been talking and now she was letting in the cold night air and telling him, 'I'll see you later. Don't wait up.'

Don't wait up he thought in frustration. If it wasn't for Alex asleep upstairs he would be going after her, bringing her back and sitting her down while he told her how he felt.

But the day was still pursuing the same irritating course it had set itself earlier when Kate had told him what her mother's friend had said, and one of the staff had interrupted the special moment of closeness they'd shared when she'd told him about Sarah buying the wedding dress.

Now, to cap it all, Kate had gone to the pub just when they had the rest of the night to themselves, and the odds were she wouldn't be rushing back.

Deep in thought he let his mind go back to when they'd

first met. They hadn't been on the best of terms during the first few days of their acquaintance, yet he'd not been able to keep away from her, and once he'd got to know Kate she'd warmed his cold heart with her kindness and compassion.

And what had he given her in return? Not a lot. Just the odd melting moment that had always ended in drawing back on his part, and must have made her feel used and insecure.

She might find it hard to believe, but she wasn't the only one who was moving on, though he might be doing it at a slower rate than she was. But he was getting there, and the last thing he needed was his own space. He wanted her, Kate, in his space for ever and always, and if in the end she tired of the uncertainty, it would serve him right.

It was boring in The Poacher's Rest, Kate thought as the evening dragged on, with village small talk all around her. She would much rather be with Daniel in the cosy sitting room at Jasmine Cottage while Alex slept safely up above.

What had she hoped to prove by coming here? That she was a free agent? If that had been the idea, she was crazy, because she wasn't. Without Daniel she would be lost.

When she got up to go, Keith, the fellow from the narrowboat who'd seen her at the surgery the other day, called across and said, 'You're not going yet, surely?'

'I'm afraid so.'

'I'll walk you home.'

She shook her head, 'No. Thanks just the same.'

He shrugged. 'Fine. Suit yourself.' And turned back to the bar.

When she arrived back at Jasmine Cottage Daniel was seated at the kitchen table, going through some paperwork that he'd brought home from the practice. He looked up and said casually, 'Did you enjoy the change of scene?'

'Not really. For one thing, your friend from the canal moorings came on to me. Wanted to walk me home.'

He frowned angrily. 'That guy has some nerve. Your mother phoned while you were out and when I told her you'd gone to the pub she said she'd ring back.'

'I'm going upstairs to hang my jacket up, so I'll phone her while I'm up there, and then I think I'll turn in,' she told him. 'It's been an exhausting day with all sorts of highs and lows, and amongst the highs were the flowers. I'm not sure if I thanked you properly for them. If I didn't, I'll say it now. Thank you.'

It sounded stilted but she couldn't help it. She wanted to know where their relationship was going, and from where she was standing the answer seemed to be nowhere. At that moment the phone rang and she dashed upstairs to answer it.

'Ah, so you're back,' her mother's voice said in her ear.

'Yes,' she informed her listlessly.

'What's wrong?'

'It's Daniel.'

'Daniel? In what way?'

'In the way that he is. He brought me flowers after we'd had a few skirmishes, and I was most ungrateful because I have a formidable rival for his affections.'

'I'm not with you,' Ruth said. 'You are in love with that delightful man and you have a rival?'

'Yes, to both questions, and to make it worse she's not of this world.'

There was a moment's silence at the other end of the line and then her mother said slowly, 'Ah, I see. It's

Lucy, the girl he was going to marry, isn't it? He can't forget her.'

'You have it in a nutshell, Mum. Why do I always have to fall in love with men who don't know their own minds?'

'It is their loss,' Ruth said comfortingly. 'Craig you are well rid of, but Daniel Dreyfus is another matter. It's to his credit that he is capable of loving so deeply, and if he ever gives his heart to another woman, it won't be without a great deal of sincerity and commitment on his part. I suggest that you ease your friendship along gently and maybe one day...'

Kate sighed. 'I can't see it happening. We were getting along famously until I fell in love with him, and now we seem more like strangers than friends.'

'Does he know you care?'

'I think he guesses and is poised for flight all the time. But enough of me. How is Gran, and is she still keen to move in with Great-Aunt Lydia?'

'Yes. I'm busy packing up for her and dealing with solicitors and estate agents. Is there any further news on Alex's father?'

'He seemed to be making good progress when we saw him over the weekend, but has still some way to go. Daniel and Alex speak to him each evening before Alex goes to bed, and the two of them are going to visit him again on Saturday.'

'So you're not going with them this time?'

'Er, no. I've decided not to. The more involved I am in Daniel's life, the more it will hurt when I'm not. In any case, it is those two that Tom will want to see, not me.'

'Does Daniel know that you're not going?'

'Not yet. I'll tell him nearer the time. I intend to go

shopping while they're gone. I need a new outfit for Sarah's wedding, and guess what? She has bought my wedding dress from the charity shop.'

'Never!'

'I'm afraid so, and the good news is I don't mind. I'm pleased that it's going to be Sarah's bridal gown, instead of it being worn by a stranger. She's thrilled to bits with it, so there we are.'

'And what about you?' her mother said. 'It is time something good happened to you.'

Kate sighed. 'Something good *has* happened, but I'm not sure how to deal with it.'

When Kate didn't come downstairs again Daniel decided to go to bed himself, but first he went to check on Alex, and when he went into his bedroom he found her standing beside his bed in a long white nightdress, looking tenderly down at the sleeping child, and as the moment took hold of him he thought that this was the kind of thing he'd been denying himself, family life. *His own family.* Lucy would not want him to deny himself a wife to cherish and children from the love they bore each other.

He'd been the one who wouldn't break faith, and until he'd met Kate it had been easy enough. But all the time he was with her she was enchanting him and feelings long dead were coming back to life.

He'd told himself she wasn't his type when they'd first met, and it had been true. She hadn't been. But that had been before he'd got the true measure of her and now she filled his every waking thought.

He reached down and straightened a cover that Alex had kicked off in sleep and when he turned to face her she'd gone noiselessly back to her own room without a word spoken between them.

It would seem that the moment hadn't got to Kate as it had to him. Maybe her being so hard to pin down during the evening had saved him from making a fool of himself.

It turned out to be a funny sort of week. Kate's enjoyment at being in general practice was increasing as her relationship with Daniel faltered. They had no problems while in the surgery. Both were keen and dedicated and they shared the workload harmoniously with Miriam, who was now a much happier person. But when their working day was over there was a constraint between them that hadn't been there before.

Amongst the rest of the staff at the practice there was the buzz of excitement that a wedding always brought, and as the event drew nearer Sarah found to her relief that the scan that Kate had arranged showed no signs of anything to be concerned about with her digestive tract.

And when Jenny announced one morning that her future son-in-law's parents had relented and would be at the wedding, Kate felt that with those two items of good news to brighten her young life, Sarah's vomiting might subside.

When she told Daniel on Thursday night that she wasn't going with them to see Tom he hid his disappointment and told himself that Kate was entitled to a life of her own, and she hadn't had much of that since she'd become bogged down with his affairs.

'Fine,' he said. 'We won't be staying overnight this time as I have appointments with a couple of people up at the house on Sunday to discuss ideas for the interior. I don't suppose you'd fancy coming along to give your opinion? It sometimes helps to have another point of view.'

'I might say the wrong thing,' she told him, and without either a yes or a no, he didn't pursue it.

On Saturday morning Kate went out onto the drive to wave Daniel and Alex off. When she'd given Alex a big hug and a kiss, and he was smiling up at her through the open window of the car, she said, 'Give my love to your dad, won't you?'

She looked at Daniel. 'As far as Mum and I are concerned, it is still on about Tom coming here to stay when the hospital discharges him, if he will accept our hospitality. She's hoping to be home soon and is looking forward to meeting him and Alex. Mum admires the way that Tom is accepting what the fates have doled out to him and is getting on with his life.'

It was a veiled rebuke for the man in the driver's seat, and as soon as she'd said it Kate wished she hadn't, but as with all words, once said they were there to stay, and the long, level look that Daniel was sending in her direction said that he'd tuned into their meaning. Without any comment he started the car and drove off.

When they disappeared from sight she went back inside and stood without moving as her mind went back down the weeks since Craig had done her the favour of pointing her in the direction of Mr Right, who at that time had been convinced he was Mr Wrong, and into the silence she said, 'I hope you approve of what is happening, Lucy. I love Daniel and know I can make him happy but, please, know that I will always respect his feelings for you.'

* * *

Alex had taken a sketching pad and coloured pencils with him to keep him occupied during the journey, and when he produced a drawing of a face with golden hair and a smiley mouth Daniel asked, 'Who is that supposed to be?'

Surprised blue eyes met his. 'Kate, of course,' his surprised youg passenger replied.

'Yes, I see,' he said, as if he didn't know, and thought that her smiles had been in short supply of late and he was responsible for that. Yet he'd been the one who'd been miserable when she'd told him she wasn't going with them. Maybe she did need some new clothes. He hoped that was the case and that she wasn't giving him some space again. Space he didn't want.

Tom's face lit up when he saw then walking down the ward towards him, but his first comment was, 'Where's Kate?'

'She couldn't make it this time,' Daniel told him, 'but she sends her love.' He noted that Tom was looking better and brighter. 'What's the news on the medical front?'

'I can manage to get about under my own steam now. Still with the help of two sticks, of course, and it is a slow process,' he informed him. 'The good news is I'm going to be discharged in a couple of weeks' time as long as I don't have any setbacks.' His expression sobered, 'In the meantime, I need to make plans for how I'm going to cope when I get home.'

He was noting Daniel's concerned expression and said reluctantly, 'Could I ask you to keep Alex for a little while longer to give me time to get used to coping before I start looking after him again?'

'I can do better than that,' he told him. 'Kate and Ruth,

her mother, want you to stay with them until you are more mobile. They have the room, and you would be back with Alex again without any stress involved.'

'That's very generous,' Tom said in amazement. 'But I couldn't possibly impose on them like that.'

'They are generous people,' he told him, thinking of the smiley curving mouth that Alex had drawn. 'They'll love having you at Jasmine Cottage. The offer of some home comforts is completely sincere.'

'Then I'll accept it,' Tom told him huskily as with moist eyes he observed his son. 'And tell them thanks from the bottom of my heart. I've been dreading how I was going to manage during the rehabilitation process and with Christmas not too far away.

'It's not my favourite time of year, though I don't let Alex see that. You aren't the only one with memories, Daniel, but you are young and free. Don't waste your life. I keep telling you she wouldn't want that.'

Her father hadn't said her name, yet they both knew who he was referring to, and once again it was Kate's face at the forefront of his mind, with Lucy smiling at him from the shadows.

CHAPTER EIGHT

AFTER a successful search for an outfit for Sarah's wedding Kate turned her attention to the more basic things and at the checkout of a supermarket found herself behind Miriam, who seemed to be stocking up with gluten-free products.

The third member of the practice was as much of a mystery to her as she was to Daniel, and remembering how he'd asked her to try to find out what was troubling her she said, 'Hi, Miriam. I'm going for a coffee when I've been served here. Do you fancy joining me?'

Surprised by her sudden appearance, Miriam said wryly. 'Why? So that you can enquire why I'm on gluten-free foods?'

'Er, no, not really. Unless you want to tell me. I know that Daniel was concerned about you at one time. He thought you mightn't be very well. But I know lots of people who eat gluten-free stuff because they like it.'

It wasn't strictly true, but she didn't want to create any waves with Miriam. She had no idea what went on in her life away from the practice, but had a feeling that it wasn't much.

'So how *is* life treating you these days, Miriam?' she asked casually when they'd found a table in a nearby coffee-bar. 'We never seem to have time to talk at the surgery, do we?'

'That's true enough,' Miriam agreed, 'but it's been much better since you came to lighten the load, and in answer to the question, life is treating me better than it was. Around the time that Daniel took over I was far from well. I recognised the symptoms, but like a lot of our patients pretended they weren't there, which was a poor showing for a doctor. But we medics are apt to think that as the dispensers of health care we're immune from life's ills.

'Anyway, to cut a long story short, I finally behaved sensibly, had the necessary tests and was diagnosed with coeliac disease and now, living a gluten-free life, I'm feeling much better, and as I've just said, having you in the practice has made a big difference to the pressure we were under.'

'Why didn't you tell Daniel you were ill?' Kate asked chidingly. 'He would have done everything he could to lighten your load.'

She shrugged narrow shoulders. 'He was already having to do that when he took over and found me to be something of a passenger.'

'But you're not now.'

'No, I'm not. And that is how I intend it to stay. So let's change the subject. Tell me what is going on in your life. I see that you still have the boy staying with you.'

'Yes. It's lovely having Alex around. I'll miss him when he goes. And what are you up to now that you're feeling better?'

The woman sitting opposite smiled. 'My sister and her family are coming to stay. I'm really looking forward to that. And there's a new man in my life too.'

'Really?'

'Yes. A four-legged one. I've acquired a delightful King Charles spaniel, who is wonderful company.'

'Good for you. What have you called him?'

'Monarch.'

'I get the connection,' Kate told her laughingly.

And with the smile still there Miriam said, 'I thought you would.'

It was late when Daniel and Alex got back and his young charge was curled up asleep in the passenger seat when Kate went out to greet them. When she opened the car door Daniel was smiling with pleasure. It was good to be back where most of his thoughts had been during the day, and he was hoping to get a smile in return when Kate heard that Tom would be delighted to stay at Jasmine Cottage for a while.

'So how was Tom?' she asked as Alex woke up and gazed around him sleepily.

It was a clear cold night with fronds of frost on the trees, and a winter moon hung over the peaks that surrounded the village. Daniel saw her shiver and said, 'Let's go inside first. This young man won't need any rocking once he's had some supper. When he's settled for the night we can talk.'

Kate nodded but didn't move. She was looking at the winter wonderland around them. 'I love this place,' she said dreamily. 'Whatever the season, it never ceases to enchant me.'

She had taken Alex by the hand and was moving towards the house and as he caught them up Daniel thought that he too was enchanted by the village, but she enchanted him more.

The memory of finding her standing beside Alex's bed in her nightdress as they'd floundered in the implications of their attraction to each other was still crystal clear. It had been a family kind of moment, but they hadn't been a family.

When Kate came downstairs after tucking a sleepy Alex under the covers she said, 'I have something to tell you about Miriam.'

'Really? What about her?'

'I met her buying gluten-free food while I was shopping in town this afternoon. She has coeliac disease. That was what was wrong with her when you took over, and she didn't want to admit it, either to you or herself.

'But now she's had the tests and is facing up to it cheerfully enough on a gluten-free diet. Also she's looking forward to having visitors which I felt might be a rarity. And wait for it—she has got herself a dog.'

'You amaze me!' he exclaimed. 'You've got more information out of Miriam in a matter of minutes than I have during all the months she and I have been working together.'

He felt a rush of bone-melting tenderness wash over him. She was so easy to love, this bright star who had come into his life so unexpectedly.

Observing him, Kate became still. It was there again, she could sense it. The sexual chemistry that was all mixed up with affection, respect and need. But what about love? Where did that come into it? Without it they wouldn't survive.

Unaware of the questions she was asking herself, he was getting back to basics. 'You asked me about Tom. He's doing well and is likely to be discharged soon. I passed on your invitation and he will be delighted to spend some time here. He was concerned about how he was going to manage when he goes home, so being here for a while will give him some breathing space.'

'That's great,' she said flatly. It was, and at any other moment she would have been sparkling across at him, but receiving the news on the tail end of another non-event in their relationship had dampened down her spirits.

'I'm going to turn in,' he told her, trying to ignore her chastened expression. 'It's been a long day and tomorrow I have a lot to see to regarding the house. Have you given any thought to what I suggested about coming along to give an opinion on the décor? I'd be glad of your help.'

At that moment the inside of his house was the last thing on his mind. He just wanted her with him. Yet there was also the thought lurking that if he asked her to marry him one day and took her to live in her favourite place in the village, she would want the house to show signs of her taste and imagination.

'Yes. I'll come if you want me to,' she said in the same flat tone, and as if the subject was closed settled herself in front of the television.

When she woke up on Sunday morning Kate's first thought was of her promise to go to the house with Daniel, and she wondered how she was going to avoid imagining herself living there with him as his wife when the prospect was so remote.

She wouldn't go back on a promise, she decided, but

would keep a very low profile and only speak when she was spoken to. *And that would be a first...*

When she went across to her bedroom window the frost of the night before was glistening on the trees and lawns of Jasmine Cottage, and not far away the bells of the old Norman church were pealing out across the countryside into the quiet Sunday morning.

It was one of the familiar, magical sounds that she'd been brought up with. Would Tom consider moving here with Alex? she wondered. The boy loved it, she could tell. Yet it didn't follow that his father would, and if she couldn't organise her own life, she was hardly equipped to organise theirs.

A knock on the door made her reach for her slippers and a robe and when she opened it, Daniel was there with tea for two on a tray decorated with sprigs of holly from the garden.

'Your room or mine?' he said warily.

'Mine,' she said in the same flat tone as the night before. 'How did you know I was awake?'

'I saw you at the window when I went out to get the holly.'

'I didn't see you.'

'Would you have wanted to?'

'Not especially.'

'That's why I kept out of sight. The tea is a peace offering after my display last night.'

'So you *did* want me?'

He groaned. 'Of course I did. But I'm not into casual sex.'

'And do you think I am?' she asked, and her voice wasn't flat any more. 'You're wrong if you do. So about you and I, then. What sort of a future have you in mind?

I've watched you with Alex, and can see that you were meant to be a family man. Don't you want children of your own?'

Her voice trailed away. A small pyjama-clad figure had appeared in the doorway, rubbing the sleep out of his eyes and murmuring, 'I'm hungry, Kate.'

She managed a smile. 'Good morning, Alex. What would you like for breakfast?'

'Cornflakes and toast, please, Kate,' he said, waking up at the thought. 'And orange juice!'

Daniel watched them go downstairs together, leaving him wishing that the day had started better.

When they arrived at the building site beneath a pale sun, Kate saw that the rooms were plastered now and the doors and windows had been glazed. The house would soon be finished and she thought that Jasmine Cottage would seem a desolate place without Daniel.

She wondered if he was anxious to move for other reasons besides the pleasure of being in his own home. Such as a desire to get away from their unavoidable closeness at the cottage.

At the surgery it wasn't so bad. There were lots of other people around and they could avoid each other if they so wished, but it wasn't so easy in the evenings and at weekends.

'So what do you think of the house?' he asked.

'It's going to be divine. You'll have everything you could want here. A brand-new home and the river, the beautiful river, at the bottom of your garden.'

'Do you envy me?'

'No, not exactly,' she replied, trying to sound casual.

'If being king of the castle without a queen is what you want.'

Alex was engrossed in skimming stones over the water and, making sure that he wasn't going to be overheard, Daniel said levelly, 'If you'd been around when Lucy died, you might understand why I'm like I am.

'She'd had the tumour removed, successfully we'd been told, and we were going ahead with our wedding plans. It was going to be a quiet affair in the circumstances with a honeymoon some time later when she felt stronger.

'Everything was arranged, with the church and the reception booked, wedding gown and bridesmaids' dresses chosen, but just one week before the big day Lucy collapsed with an embolism, a blood clot that had suddenly manifested itself, and she never regained consciousness. So, you see, yours wasn't the only wedding dress that there was suddenly no use for.'

'What did you do with it?' she asked, a lump in her throat.

'Took it back to the shop.'

'So you'd done it before when I asked you to take mine.'

'Yes. Something like it.'

'I would never have asked if I'd known,' she told him contritely.

'You've already told me that and I believe you, so don't feel bad about it. But now do you understand me better?'

She nodded without speaking. It was as if what he'd just said had put any chance of him loving *her* out of the question, and she wanted to run away to hide her hurt, but a strange person had appeared in the tearful blur before her eyes and it was time to gather her wits and be supportive.

The interior designer had arrived and as Daniel and she shook hands Kate went to call Alex away from the river-bank, and the four of them went into the cold shell of the house together.

When they were back home and preparing the evening meal Daniel came to stand beside her. Looking down at her bent head as she chopped vegetables for a stir-fry, he asked, 'What did you think of the suggestions we received?'

'Hmm. They were good,' she murmured. 'You didn't need me.'

'I don't agree. Were the colour schemes and fabrics what you would have chosen?'

'Some of them were. Others weren't.'

'Jot down those you liked and those you weren't keen on and I'll see what I think the next time I'm there.'

He wanted to tell her that all the time they'd been talking to the interior decorator from one of the large furnishing companies in the nearest town, he'd been imagining what it would be like to have Kate there for evermore beside him. Filling it with her vibrancy. Bringing it to life with her presence.

He'd imagined her holding a golden-haired baby in her arms and smiling down at a small dark-haired girl close by her side. But in the picture *he'd* been standing to one side, grave and unapproachable, and he'd known that he wasn't there yet.

Monday was always busy at the surgery and on the following day it was busier than usual with seasonal ailments and people who'd come to grief on icy pavements.

So far there had been no snow to the disappointment of the children and the relief of older folk who knew how treacherous the road across the moors could be in such weather.

But the icy conditions were persisting and when Kate discovered that Jane Appleton had asked for a home visit, she was reminded of when she'd worked at the surgery previously and the elderly widow had been found with hypothermia in her remote cottage in a gully between the peaks after being cut off for a week in blizzard conditions.

She had recovered and refused to move to a less hazardous location in spite of advice from all sides. Now Jane had been brought to mind once more as she'd requested a home visit.

She must be over eighty by now, Kate thought, and from her records it appeared that the stoic elderly widow hadn't seen a doctor since the blizzard episode. But now she was needing one and had done the sensible thing by asking for a visit instead of venturing out onto the icy roads.

The gritting lorry would have been out on the road up to the moors because heavy traffic sometimes used it to shorten the journey to Sheffield, but Jane's cottage was not the easiest of places to get to and the lorry didn't go that far.

'This house call to a Jane Appleton,' Daniel said at the end of morning surgery. 'I don't recognise the address. Would you know where she lives?'

Kate nodded. 'Yes, only too well. Jane lives in an isolated spot on the edge of the moors. She was once snowed in there with what could have been disastrous results. Afterwards we all tried to persuade her to move but she wouldn't budge.

'Her husband, Reuben, was a shepherd on one of the

hill farms, and she's lived at Gorse Brow Cottage ever since they married. He died some years ago and she lives there alone now. Jane is a hardy old soul but…'

'Exactly,' he said dryly. 'Time marches on, and it sounds as if the lady might not be as fit as she was. She's complaining of severe pain in the hips so I'm going to make her my first call.'

'I'll go if you like,' she said,

Daniel shook his head. 'Not in these weather conditions.'

'I know the terrain better than you do.'

'Then why don't we both go? It will be an ideal opportunity for me to expand my knowledge of it. This is my first winter in these parts and I'm realising that the countryside can be dangerous as well as breathtaking.'

'I hope the weather behaves itself for Sarah's wedding,' she said. 'I've bought a pale blue winter suit and some matching calf-high boots, and for the evening I've got a long black dress that I've been saving for something like that.' She smiled before continuing, 'I bought Alex a smart jacket and trousers while I was shopping on Saturday and luckily they're a good fit, so with one of his better shirts and a smart little tie he's sorted. What do you intend wearing?'

'I don't know, Kate,' he said sombrely. 'I'm more concerned about what Sarah will be wearing and if you really are ready to see her in it.'

'I will be,' she told him steadily. 'I thought you understood that I've moved on. *I'm* not in a time warp. I'll be fine.'

And that's one for me, he thought as they went out into the cold together. Another reminder that if *my* life is standing still, Kate's isn't.

* * *

Even before he'd examined her Daniel could tell that Jane Appleton needed two new hips, and to have to tell her that at eighty-five years old was a daunting thought. 'I'm going to arrange for you to see a consultant at the hospital, Mrs Appleton,' he told her. 'You have quite advanced arthritis in both hips, from what I can see.'

She was a big buxom woman for her age, which might be fortunate with regard to stamina, but he was aware that it could be partly the weight she was carrying that had caused the hips to be so troublesome.

Jane took it all quite calmly. 'I can't grumble,' she said. 'Apart from that time when I was snowed up and thought I'd got frostbite, I've never ailed much. That was the worst winter we'd had for a long time and there's been none like it since.'

'How about moving nearer civilisation?'

She shook her head. 'No. Here I've lived ever since my Reuben was taken, and here I'll die.'

'And what if this winter should turn out to be like the one you mentioned and we doctors can't get up here to attend you?'

'I'll take my chances,' she said stoutly. She smiled at Kate. 'Can I offer you folks a cup of tea and a slice of homemade cake before you go?'

They were ready to leave and Daniel was shaking his head, so Kate told her, 'Thank you, Jane, but no. We'd love to stop awhile but we still have some calls to make. The demand for our services increases rapidly at this time of year.'

As he drove away towards places that would be less hazardous to find Daniel was thinking that the patient they had just left might need to have a rethink about where she was going to spend the rest of her days, if her mobility got any worse.

When they separated back at the surgery Kate went to see the eyes and ears of the village, her mother's friend, Frances. She'd received the hospital's report on the tests that she'd sent her for and it had shown that she had non-Hodgkin's lymphoma to a degree that was treatable.

Knowing that Frances would have already been told the results by the consultant she'd seen, Kate was concerned that she hadn't been to the surgery to discuss them in her usual forthright manner.

When Frances opened the door to her she knew the reason why. The driving force that had always kept her at the forefront of village affairs was missing. She looked pale and drawn.

'I suppose you've come to tell me you've had the report from the hospital,' she said listlessly as she stepped back to let Kate into the house.

'Yes, I have,' she said gently, 'and I am so sorry that they have worrying news for you, Frances.'

'I've got non-Hodgkin's lymphoma,' she said in the same toneless sort of voice.

'Yes,' Kate agreed, marvelling that a woman of such strength of character should be so demoralised. 'But the hospital have said that it is treatable with radiotherapy, haven't they, Frances? That the disease is confined to just one group of lymph nodes, which makes the outlook more promising.'

'But what about all my committees?' she wailed. 'How will they manage without me? I haven't time to be ill. If the treatment makes me too poorly to attend all the meetings that I chair, or worse still if I die from this thing, they will be in chaos. You know that everyone relies on me.'

'It's your health that is the most important thing now,' Kate said, firmly but gently. 'Concentrate on getting better, and I'm sure there'll be someone who can cover for you while you are having treatment.' She marvelled even more at the strange attitude of the woman sitting opposite her. Surely she wasn't more concerned about her standing in the community than her health. But as she'd never had husband or children to fill her days, maybe it wasn't so strange after all.

'When is your mother coming home?' Frances asked fractiously. 'I miss her.'

'Soon, very soon,' she soothed. 'My gran is going to live with her sister now that she's much better, and Mum is dealing with the move. As long as there are no hiccups she should be home in two to three weeks.

'Also we're expecting young Alex's father coming to stay with us. He's due to be discharged from hospital soon, with the thought hanging over him that he might never be able to walk unaided again.'

'Hmm,' Frances said dismissively, own concerns uppermost in her mind. 'So now I have to wait for an appointment for the radiotherapy, do I?

'Yes, it shouldn't be long, and in the meantime try to think positively, as you've always done, Frances. Just carry on chairing your committees and keeping to your daily routine. Remember that we at the surgery are always there for you.'

How ever did her mother cope with Frances? Kate

wondered as she drove away from the house. It was fortunate that Ruth had lots of patience and a sense of
humour.

At two o'clock the following afternoon Alex's class was
doing a play for their parents in the school hall, and as
both of them wanted to be there Miriam had agreed to
hold the fort at the surgery while they went to watch his
stage debut.

As they walked the short distance to the school, Kate
thought that this was the part of their lives that was
problem-free, looking after Alex, and as she observed the
strong profile of the man beside her she wasn't aware that
Daniel's thoughts were running along the same lines.

They were part of the throng of parents and grandpar-
ents going to watch their children perform, he was
thinking, and wished that Alex belonged to them. But the
fact remained that he didn't. He was Tom's son, and with
every passing day he was realising what he was missing
out on.

He ached for Kate and the life they could have
together, but there was a dread inside him that he might
cause her hurt if he found that he couldn't live up to any
promises he made.

Strolling along beside him, with her cheeks rosy from
the cold and the anticipation of what was to come at the
school giving a spring to her step, she seemed content
enough, but was she? The attraction between them was
strong, with desire always just below the surface. But
they had both been involved in painful situations.

For Kate there had been the broken engagement that
she seemed to be shrugging off so successfully on the

outside, but it didn't stop Daniel from wondering if her feelings for him were part of her being on the rebound.

As for his side of it, he had been forced to bear the pain of all pains and it had changed him for ever. Neither of them had met as free spirits and how he wished they had.

CHAPTER NINE

WHEN the young actors came trooping onto the stage in the assembly hall, the two doctors exchanged smiles as Alex's glance searched the audience until he found them a few rows from the front, and then he was smiling too.

As the story of the play unfolded, Kate and Daniel saw that not only was Alex a capable young artist, he could also act. Obviously their young charge was going to excel at the arts.

Daniel had taken his camera as Tom wasn't able to see his son in the play, but at least when next they visited him they would have photographs to show him.

When it was over and the senior girls and teachers were bringing around refreshments, Graham, the headmaster, came to have a word with them.

'Alex is doing fine,' he said. 'We'll be sorry to lose him.'

'So will we,' Kate told him, 'but it seems that he might be with us longer than we expected.'

'It's a difficult situation,' Daniel explained. 'Alex's father is facing an uncertain future from shattered knee joints and may not be very mobile for a long time, but he's anxious to be back with his son. He's coming to Jasmine Cottage for a while when they discharge him from hospital, so we're pleased that Alex won't be leaving us yet.'

'Can we take him back with us now to save one of us having to return later?' Kate asked the headmaster.

He nodded. 'Yes. School is over for today.'

It was the last Saturday of the month, the day of Sarah's wedding to her childhood sweetheart, and as the organist began to play the wedding march to announce to the crowded village church that the bride had arrived, Daniel was observing Kate anxiously.

He wasn't convinced that she could cope with this. Supposing she was intending putting on an act for Sarah's sake, having told her where the wedding dress had come from. Many of those there were turning to see what the bride looked like, but Kate was sitting quite still beside him.

Until, holding tightly onto her father's arm, Sarah drew level with them. It was then that Kate turned her head and as the glances of the bride-to-be and the bride-not-to-be met, she smiled her brilliant smile. Sarah beamed back at her, and he knew then that Kate really had moved on, and if he didn't watch it, she might 'move on' straight past him.

Alex's friend Scott and his parents were amongst the guests. Apparently they were related to Jenny's husband, and when the ceremony was over and they were all making their way to the village hall for the reception, Alex said, 'Scott has invited me to a sleepover at his house tonight. Can I go?'

'What do you think, Kate?' Daniel asked. 'Do you think we should let him go? They seem a decent family, but Alex *is* in our care.'

She nodded. 'Maybe you should check it out with his parents first, just to make sure it isn't something that Scott has dreamed up himself.'

Daniel came back smiling. 'The Thompsons know all about it. There won't be a houseful, just the two boys, so I've said yes, much to Alex's delight. They'll take him home with them after the evening reception.' *And we will have Jasmine Cottage to ourselves he thought, but didn't put it into words.*

When they went home in the late afternoon to get changed for the evening ahead, Alex went upstairs to play with his games until it was time to go, and Daniel picked up the phone to ring Tom to confirm that the three of them would be visiting him the following day when they'd collected Alex from the sleepover.

While they were both involved with their own affairs, Kate planted herself on the sofa in the sitting room for a quiet moment.

There was a deep feeling of release inside her. She'd kept her promise to Sarah and had let her see clearly that she had no problems whatsoever at seeing her in the dress.

If she had found freedom from the past, how far off was Daniel from finding it? she wondered. His had been a much deeper commitment than hers and one that had been ended by circumstance rather than choice.

At that moment he appeared and when she heard what he had to say she understood the surprise in his expression.

'Tom says he can come out tomorrow. I've arranged to go and fetch him, so we'll need to change the bedrooms round and prepare for his arrival.'

'That's great news!' she exclaimed. 'And much, much sooner than we expected.'

'The hospitals seem to be speeding up the process after surgery and discharging patients the moment they are fit to go,' he commented dryly. 'Tom isn't complaining and Alex will be thrilled.'

'Yes,' she agreed. 'All we need now is Mum back where she belongs.'

He nodded and then said in a low voice, 'About Sarah's wedding and the dress. I was proud of you. When she appeared I was panicking that you mightn't be up to seeing her in it, but I should have known that, having given your word, you would carry it through.'

The wedding dress is my past, she thought, and you are my future, if only you would see it that way. But he only saw in part, and the part that he saw wasn't why she'd coped so well at the church.

When she came downstairs in the long black dress that offset the honey gold of her hair, the two of them were waiting for her in the hall.

'You look stunning,' Daniel said as he opened the front door. 'This is the first time we've been out together in the evening socially, isn't it?'

'Yes,' she agreed, 'and if the narrowboat guy is there, please don't let him near me.'

'That problem can be solved by you having every dance with me,' he teased, but as the evening progressed she realised that he'd meant it. While Alex and the other young ones watched a conjuror in another room they danced every dance together. People were staring but Kate didn't care. She was in Daniel's arms and nothing else mattered.

After the Thompson family had left, taking Alex with them, Kate and Daniel said their goodbyes to Jenny and her husband and set off for home.

Sarah and Jason had left earlier to begin their honeymoon and as they had left, Sarah had whispered to Kate, 'I haven't been sick once in the last few days.'

'Brilliant!' she'd said as they'd exchanged conspiratorial smiles. 'You're going to be fine.' And now as they drove away from the village hall the two doctors were both very much aware that they had the night ahead to themselves.

'This must be how parents feel when they pass their children over to a relative, or some form of childminder for a while,' Daniel said with a quirky smile, and Kate nodded dreamily.

She'd had a lovely evening in his arms on the dance floor and it had been made complete by Sarah's news that she was fully recovered. Now it could only get better.

At that moment she wasn't to know that her contentment was to be short-lived. To get to Jasmine Cottage they had to pass the end of the lane where Furzebank, the rest home for the elderly, was situated, and Daniel said, 'Am I seeing things, or is something on fire down there?'

When Kate swivelled sideways in her seat she cried, 'You aren't seeing things and the only property down there is the rest home.'

Turning quickly off the main road, he drove in the direction of where flames and smoke were rising into the night sky, and when they pulled up outside the rest home, where thirty old folk were living out their remaining years, they saw that it was on fire.

As they flung themselves out of the car they could see Helen, the sister-in-charge, along with a couple of night staff, helping them out of the building in their night-clothes. When she saw them Helen cried hoarsely, 'Saints be praised! Where have you two doctors appeared from?'

'We were in the area and saw the blaze,' Daniel said, 'so what's the situation? Is everybody out, and have you sent for the emergency services?'

She nodded. 'Yes to ambulances and the fire services. They are on their way. No to everybody being out. Tommy Simpson has barricaded himself into his room and won't come out, and the rest are going to die from pneumonia from the cold, or breathing difficulties from the smoke, if we don't get them to somewhere warm and safe soon.'

Kate had picked up Daniel's doctor's bag as they'd leapt out of the car and was already busy amongst the residents, checking for cuts and bruises or signs of acute distress, and he called across, 'Put as many as you can in my car, Kate, and in any other vehicles lying around, and I'll go and get Tommy. What room is he in?' he asked Helen urgently.

'Number twenty-nine,' she shrieked above the distressed cries of the old folk. 'It's at the other end of the building on the first floor. Furthest away from the staircase and the lift.'

Kate was beside him, her face ashen with fear. 'Wait for the fire services, Daniel,' she pleaded. 'It's too dangerous to go in there.'

'There's no sign of them so far,' he said. 'I have to, Kate.'

'Then I'm coming with you.'

'No! You are not! You can do more good out here. See to the others. I won't be long.'

'Don't do this to me,' she cried. 'Help will be here any moment.'

'It could be a moment too late,' he told her, and throwing off her grasp he disappeared into the building...

Tommy's room would be at the other end of the building, Daniel thought as he fought his way up the smoke-filled staircase, and as he ran along the upstairs corridor with his handkerchief over nose and mouth he wondered why on earth the old guy wouldn't let them in. Maybe he was too frightened to come out.

'Tommy!' he yelled, banging on the door of number twenty nine. 'It's Dr Dreyfus. I've come to get you. Let me in!'

There was no reply and when he looked down smoke was seeping from under the door, so there was nothing else for it but to put his shoulder against it and hope that whatever was jamming it would give, as for obvious reasons none of the doors had locks.

It took a few attempts before it opened and the chair that the old man had jammed beneath the handle gave way. When he flung himself inside Daniel found Tommy in a heap in the middle of the floor. He was a small scrap of a man so he picked him up easily enough and then turned to make the return journey through the smoke and licking flames.

By the time he got to the top of the stairs he could hear the sound of a fire engine down below and almost in the same second the fire crew was in the building, running up the stairs towards him.

Tommy had stopped breathing by the time they got him

outside, and the paramedics who'd arrived just before the fire crew rushed forward to give resuscitation. It took some minutes before his frail form responded to their efforts and, knowing that his heart and lungs might stop functioning again because of smoke inhalation, no time was wasted in lifting him on board for a fast transfer to A and E at the nearest hospital, with a second ambulance following behind with one of the old ladies who'd had a heart attack.

When Daniel had come out of the building, smoke blackened, breathless, but alive, Kate thought she would faint with relief as she ran towards him.

He had propped himself against the side of the fire engine and was coughing and gasping for breath, but he managed a smile, his teeth showing whitely in the grime on his face.

'Don't try to talk,' she said gently, as the terror began to recede before a huge tide of thankfulness. 'You really are quite something, you know.'

Ignoring her advice not to talk, he croaked, '*You* would have done the same if I hadn't been here.'

She shuddered. 'I'm not so sure about that!'

'I am,' he wheezed, and she eyed him anxiously,

'I think you need to be checked over in A and E.'

'Maybe, but give me time for my airway to settle down and I'll see how I am then.' He looked around him. 'What's the situation with the rest of the old folk?'

She managed a smile. 'Miraculously they seem to have come through the ordeal safely. The vicar and some of the villagers have arrived with hot-water bottles and blankets and are taking them in convoy to the village hall for the night until proper temporary accommodation can be found for them.'

'How did the vicar and his flock know what was happening?' he asked as his breathing improved.

'Village grapevine, bush telegraph, or whatever you want to call it, and a blaze like that in the night sky is not to be missed.'

A couple of hours later the fire crew were satisfied that the blaze, which had been confined to the upper floor, was completely extinguished and now they were searching through the debris for anything that could have started it.

The residents had all been transferred safely with Helen and her assistants in charge, and satisfied that the emergency was over the paramedics had returned to base.

Which left just the two doctors, and once they were satisfied that all that could be done for the old folk had been done, Kate drove them back home.

She was relieved to see that Daniel was breathing more easily and as if reading her thoughts, he said, 'I'm not as breathless now. I'll see how am I in the morning but I don't think it will be necessary to go to A and E. I was only in there a matter of minutes.'

She shuddered. 'It seemed like an eternity to me.'

'I'm sorry that I put you through that,' he said gravely, taking in the pallor of her face and the crumpled black dress beneath her jacket. 'But it was a no-choice situation, Kate, and I can't think of anyone I would rather have had with me at that moment than you. We're a good team, you and I.'

'Like Batman and Robin to the rescue,' she said with a tired smile.

'Not exactly. But we'll discuss that another time when *you* aren't so tired and *I* don't look as if I've just done a shift down the pit.'

* * *

The clock in the sitting room showed half past four as Kate went to make a pot of tea, and as she stood at the sink, watching the kettle fill, it seemed like a lifetime since they'd been driving contentedly home from the wedding reception, looking forward to some time to themselves.

Instead, they'd spent the last few hours with the residents and staff from the home, the emergency services and half the village, and now the only thought in her mind was to curl up in bed and go to sleep.

When they'd drunk the tea Daniel said, 'I'm going up to wash the grime off me, Kate.' He patted her cheek gently. 'I hope you don't have a nightmare after the happenings of the last few hours.'

'I've had it already,' she told him sombrely. 'I don't ever again want to have to live through a moment as terrifying as when you disappeared into the smoke and flames.'

He held her close for the briefest of moments. 'It's over. Forget it. Go and get some sleep while I remove the smell of the fire.' And because she was exhausted she didn't argue.

But sleep wasn't quick in coming. She heard him come out of the bathroom, go downstairs and start opening cupboard doors. What on earth was he looking for? she wondered, and decided that the best thing to do was go downstairs and find out.

She didn't need to ask. When Daniel turned round and she saw the blistered skin on his forearm, the answer was there.

'Hi,' he said. 'I'm looking to see if we have a first-aid box.'

'It's on the top shelf in the pantry,' she said. 'And if

there aren't any antiseptic burn dressings in it, I've got some in my bag in the car.'

There weren't, and as she opened the door to go outside he said, 'I'll go and get them, Kate. You aren't dressed for being out in the cold night air.'

She turned slowly and fixed him with a steady blue gaze. 'Why is it that you are always so ready to help everyone you meet, Daniel, but never want to be on the receiving end of the care and kindness of others?

'Too much independence can be hurtful. I know where it stems from, of course. You live by the rule of no involvement, no hurt. I'm quite capable of going to get the burn dressings and I can't believe that you didn't ask me to dress it for you before.'

He sighed. 'You're right in all you say but, then, you usually are. I just didn't want to disturb you after the night we've had, and it wasn't until I'd washed off the grime that I saw the blisters.'

She hadn't heard him. Kate had picked up her car keys off the hall table and was out on the drive, foraging in the back seat of her car for the case.

'I can't believe that you didn't feel this hurting,' she said gently as she dressed the burn a few minutes later.

'I did, but I was so concerned about what was going on with Tommy and the old folk, there was no time to start fussing over it.' He gave a wry smile. 'If that sounds like another example of the independence that you described, I can't help it.'

At that moment he'd never felt less independent in his life. He needed her like he needed to breathe. Her touch was like a touch he'd always known. Her nearness the promise of an end to loneliness.

He was ready to throw off the mantle of the independence she'd described, but there had to be a better time than this to tell her so. A time when they were not exhausted and traumatised at the end of a terrible night.

'As your doctor I'm suggesting that you sleep on the opposite side to the burn,' she said with assumed authority when she'd finished, 'and that I fetch you a drink of water and then help you up to bed.'

'Only if you are going to join me there,' he said laughingly, putting his more serious thoughts to one side for the moment. 'I'm quite capable of doing those other things myself, but it takes two for what I might have in mind.'

She didn't join in the laughter. 'You're saying that because of what I said earlier. If our relationship ever becomes what I long for it to be, it will because you feel the same as I do, not because you are trying to be something you aren't. Go to bed…on your own…you adorable man,' she said softly, and planting a butterfly kiss on his cheek she went up the stairs before him, got into bed and slept.

The fire of the night before was the first thought in their minds when the two doctors woke up after just a few hours' sleep the next morning, and after a phone call to the Thompson household to explain that they would be at the village hall during the morning if they wanted to drop Alex off there, they made their way to where the residents of Furzebank had spent the night.

Kate had put a fresh dressing on Daniel's burn before they'd left and this time it had been an impersonal affair. They were about to put the needs of others before their closeness of the night before.

* * *

When they arrived at the village hall, Social Services staff were there organising temporary care for the homeless old folk, and while they were waiting to be moved, Kate and Daniel checked them over for bronchial and heart problems. Some were very frail and they were concerned that the smoke from the fire and being taken out into the cold the night before might have affected them.

On the face of it there seemed to be no cause for any of them to be hospitalised, but the thought was in both their minds that the situation could change at any time.

The sister had calmed down once she knew they were all safe, including Tommy, but the news on him wasn't good. He was in Intensive Care and very poorly.

A photographer from the local paper was there wanting a picture of the hero of the hour, but Daniel said, 'No, thanks. I only did what anyone else would have done.'

'What did you do, Uncle Dan?' Alex asked. He'd just been dropped off and was gazing around him wide-eyed.

'Nothing,' he told him, ruffling his dark locks,

'I'll tell you what Dr Dreyfus did,' the sister said. 'He went into the burning building and rescued one of my patients. The old man had locked himself in a smoke-filled room and he had to break down the door to get to him.'

When Daniel glanced at Kate there were tears on her lashes and he knew that she must have thought that he might not come out alive. It was humbling to know that someone could care for him so much

Alex was experiencing no such feelings but, then, *he* had no reason to. 'Wait till I tell Scott!' he cried, with visions of his playground credibility improving by leaps and bounds.

* * *

At last the hall was empty. The residents had been taken to their new homes and, bereft of their charges, the staff from Furzebank had gone back to view the damage.

The fire service was still inspecting the property for the cause of the blaze and were having discussions with council representatives who had been summoned to the scene, as it seemed as if the wiring of the building could be suspect.

Despite his exhaustion, Daniel still had to fetch Tom, and night was wrapped around the village as he drove along the main street in the direction of Jasmine Cottage. Tom, who had been dozing in the passenger seat, had woken up and was slowly stretching his legs and observing with interest the quaint shops and limestone cottages

'They look more cheerful than that place of mine, don't they?' he said wryly, and although he didn't comment Daniel had to agree. They'd gone to the tidy semi-detached where Tom lived with Alex in a quiet Gloucestershire street to pick up clothes and other necessities that he would need during the coming weeks, and there had been an unlived-in look about it.

It wasn't surprising as it had been empty for weeks and now, by comparison, Tom's first glimpse of the village was of glistening frost on the trees and grasses, and the lamplit windows of the houses.

'I can see why you like living here,' he said. 'All this, and Kate, too.'

'I wish,' he told the man who he'd once thought would be his father-in-law. 'The village asks nothing of me except that I look after the health of its inhabitants, but Kate is a different matter.

'When we first met she was reeling from a broken engagement, and there has always been anxiety at the back of my mind that she might be on the rebound. Though she did ask me to take her wedding dress to the charity shop. But that worry has gone. A girl from the village was married in the dress yesterday and Kate was fine about it, quite pleased, in fact. But we have another ongoing problem that isn't proving so easy to solve. When we first met I was still mourning Lucy, had never thought of putting anyone in her place, and I made it clear when Kate showed an interest in me.

'Now I need to convince her that I'm ready to move on. That Lucy is my past, and *she* is my present. But I keep getting sidetracked and the fact that I allow that to happen makes me wonder if I'm being fair to her. In a nutshell, I think Kate could do better than me.'

Tom shook his head. 'Never! I'm not going to let you say that! You had a raw deal when you lost Lucy and I'm delighted that you've found someone else to love. It doesn't mean that because we've been getting on with our lives Alex and I loved Lucy any the less, and I've always wanted you to see it that way.

'From what I've seen of Kate and heard of her mother, they are very special people. I'm looking forward to meeting Ruth and am sure that Kate's generosity of spirit will allow for your memories of Lucy.'

Jasmine Cottage was in sight. There was no more time for giving voice to his innermost thoughts to the man by his side. He just wished that Kate was as easily convinced that he was ready to move on as Tom was.

As he stopped the car the cottage door was flung open and they were there. Alex jumping up and down with excitement as his father eased himself slowly out of the car and balanced himself on two crutches, and Kate beaming her welcome.

The driveway was displaying a fine film of ice and Daniel took Tom's arm to give him extra support as he moved slowly towards them, and then they were all inside.

Leaving father and son to enjoy their special moment, the two doctors went into the kitchen where a casserole was waiting to be served and an apple crumble was browning nicely in the oven.

'So getting Tom here safely is plan A accomplished,' he said. 'Are you happy about that?'

'Yes, of course I am,' she said brightly. 'It's great to see them together.'

'And tomorrow plan B will fall into place. Your mother will be home at last. But what about plan C? You and I?' he questioned carefully.

'What about it?' she said levelly, and went into the sitting room to announce that the meal was ready.

It was a light-hearted affair on everyone's part except Daniel's. Kate was going to give up on him, he thought. She was weary of all the affection being on her side and she wasn't to know that if it hadn't been for the fire at Furzebank the previous night, he'd been going to ask her to marry him.

But nothing had gone to plan and afterwards he had decided that before he proposed to her he was going to have a ring to put on her finger...*if she said yes.*

With that in mind he'd stopped off at a large jeweller's in the town on his way to pick Tom up and now had a solitaire diamond in small box in his pocket, waiting for the moment when he had Kate to himself for once.

They'd had a rethink regarding rearranging the bedrooms to accommodate Tom. Instead, they'd cleared out the study at the end of the hall and turned it into a bedroom so that he would have no need to climb the stairs. There was a toilet and shower room next to it so he would be able to stay at ground level all the time he was with them.

After what must have been an exhausting day for him he'd gone to bed as soon as an excited Alex had finally drifted off, and once the two of them were alone Daniel said, 'We need to talk, Kate.'

'Is that so?' she said coolly.

He sighed. Today had been his first chance to buy the ring. He hadn't had a moment to spare from the surgery since then to go shopping and was about to explain when she had him groaning in dismay.

'I'm afraid that my stay in the village is going to be short,' she said. 'I'm going to move on to somewhere where I can regain my sanity.'

He was appalled and now there was anger in him. 'So you're going to let us down at the practice, then,' he said tightly, picking on the thing that mattered least. It was the thought of her disappearing from his life that was like a knife thrust.

'Not until you've replaced me.' Kate replied stiffly.

'You're crazy! This place is where you should be. Not in some other general practice or living in hospital accommodation somewhere.'

'I'll be the judge of that.'

'Yes, I'm sure you will. But I have a better idea. *I'll* go and leave *you* where you belong.'

'No! You can't do that,' she said hastily. 'I don't want to drive you away. What about your beautiful house, and Tom and Alex?'

'There are "beautiful houses" in other places. With regard to Tom and Alex, I'm not their keeper. Tom is quite capable of managing his own affairs now that he's becoming mobile again. He said in the car that his firm has offered him early retirement and he's going to take them up on it. So that will make life less complicated for them both.'

'But Alex loves it here,' Kate reminded him.

'Yes, I know, but it was never meant to be permanent. How could it be?'

Her world was falling apart around her, Kate was thinking. She'd mentioned leaving the village to see how Daniel would react and had obviously said the wrong thing.

'I wanted to do some shopping before we talked again,' he said, 'and on my way to pick Tom up was the first opportunity.'

'Shopping!' she said incredulously. 'What kind of shopping?'

'This sort of shopping. Hold out your hand.' He took the box with the ring in it out of his pocket and placed it on her open palm.

'It's meant to be worn on just one particular finger,' he said evenly, 'so don't consider wearing it anywhere else just to please me, Kate. Only put it on if you mean it. I can't believe that after all we've achieved together you would disappear from my life just like that. I'll see you in the morning. Goodnight.'

When he'd gone she stood motionless in anguished astonishment with the box still unopened on her palm, then followed him slowly up the stairs and didn't open it until she was in her bedroom with the door shut.

CHAPTER TEN

RUTH was home and delighted to be so. She had met Tom and Alex, and when Kate popped home from the surgery in the lunch-hour to make sure she had arrived safely she found them getting along famously.

After mother and daughter had held each other close in happy reunion Ruth said, 'There's bad weather on the way for tomorrow. We've just seen the weather report and heavy snow and gale-force winds are forecast for these parts.'

'Oh, no!' Kate exclaimed, and turned to Tom. 'When it snows around here the road through Woodhead Pass is blocked at the first fall. Folk who live up near the tops are often snowed in for days until it thaws.'

Ruth was observing the daughter that she knew so well and could tell that Kate was not her usual bouncy self. She was pale and looked tired, as if she wasn't sleeping well.

There was something wrong, she could tell it a mile off. But any questions would have to wait until later in the day when they had a moment to themselves. She'd been hoping to come home to find that Kate had finally found the man of her dreams, but it wasn't looking like that.

That evening as they all sat around the dinner table Ruth said, 'This is wonderful, having my lovely home filled with special people. It's been an empty place for me since Kate's father died and she went to work away.' She smiled at Alex. 'We've even got some young blood amongst us, and if we aren't too happy about the snow that's on its way, I know that he is.'

'Yes!' he cried, and turning to Kate who was sitting next to him, 'Will you and Uncle Dan help me to make a snowman, Kate?'

'Of course we will,' she said, giving him a squeeze, and as he watched them, Tom's eyes were moist. He could tell from the way he talked about her that Alex loved her. That without presuming in any way she had taken Lucy's place in his life, and he was grateful. She had also taken Lucy's place in Daniel's life and he prayed that she would give him the love and tenderness that he so much deserved.

Daniel was sitting opposite her and had never taken his glance off her since the moment they'd both arrived home from the surgery, but Tom had noticed there had been no conversation between them, and if Kate was aware of Daniel's preoccupation with her, she wasn't showing it.

Later in the evening, when Alex was asleep and the men had gone to their own rooms, Ruth went to have the chat with Kate that she had promised herself.

'What's wrong?' she asked the moment they were closeted in her bedroom.

'I've really messed everything up with Daniel,' Kate said with her usual directness.

'In what way?'

'Lack of understanding. Being too pushy. Lots of things. Last night I told him I was leaving the village because we weren't getting anywhere, and guess what? He had a beautiful engagement ring in his pocket.'

'And?'

'He gave it to me, still in the box, and as good as told me not to wear it unless I'd got my act together.'

'And have you?' her mother asked gently.

'No. Not really. I feel as if I've badgered him into giving it to me.'

'So it's stalemate.'

'Yes. That describes it exactly,' Kate said dolefully.

'That may be,' Ruth commented, 'but his gaze was on you all the time we were having dinner tonight.'

'It would be Alex he was looking at, sitting next to me. He dotes on him,' she said, not to be comforted.

'So now you have the chance to give him some children of his own to love.'

'You wouldn't think so if you'd heard him when he thrust the ring at me,' she told her. 'He never said he loved me.'

'Did you give him the chance?' her mother asked gently.

'Er, maybe not, but…'

'What have you done with it?'

'It's in the drawer of the dressing-table,' she said listlessly, 'and it's beautiful. Do you want to see it?'

Ruth shook her head. 'Not until it's on your finger.'

But what if that never happened? Kate thought sadly.

The next morning the snow that had been forecast had arrived and, as promised, it had brought a strong, biting wind with it that would not let it settle, so that it was drifting up against fences and railings as the two doctors drove to the surgery in their separate cars.

Alex's last words as Kate had dropped him off at school had been, 'Don't forget we are going to make a snowman when we get home.'

'I won't forget,' she'd promised, and had wished her relationship with Daniel was as uncomplicated as when she was with Alex.

It was a vain hope that they might have a quiet morning, with the snow keeping people indoors. The waiting room was full and kept refilling, and in a miserable sort of way Kate was glad.

So far the only conversation between Daniel and herself had been about practice matters and that she could cope with.

As the weather worsened steadily he suggested to Miriam that she go home as her house was in the next village, and if she stayed until the end of the day, the roads might be impassable.

She didn't refuse and, having tidied up all the loose ends regarding her patients, she left with all speed, leaving Kate and Daniel to deal with house calls and the afternoon surgery. Fortunately only one visit had been requested, to a farm not too far away, and at the end of the morning Daniel went to deal with it.

He had only been gone a matter of minutes when another request came through to Kate. It was from Jane Appleton in the remote cottage that they'd visited not so long ago in much better weather, and this time the elderly woman was in great distress.

'It's Jane Appleton here,' a voice quavered in her ear. 'I need a doctor urgently. Is anyone available?'

'Er, yes,' Kate said. 'I am, Mrs Appleton. What is the problem?'

'When I got out of bed this morning the room began to spin round and I'm so dizzy I can't keep my balance. I've been on the floor twice.'

'Stay where you are. Don't move until I get there,' she told her. 'What's the weather like where you are?'

'Not good,' she said weakly. 'Have you got a shovel?'

'I most certainly have,' Kate told her. 'I've lived in these parts too long not to respect the weather in winter. I'll be with you shortly.

'I'm going to Jane Appleton's place out in the wilds,' she told Jenny as she flung on her long winter coat. 'Will you tell Daniel when he gets back? I'm hoping not to be long with the weather being what it is, but it all depends on how long it takes me to get there, and how ill she is when I do.'

She gave her mother a quick ring before she set off to explain where she was going, and Ruth said worriedly, 'Daniel won't want you out there in this weather and neither do I.'

'I can't help that,' she said wryly. 'Our patients don't become ill according to how the weather is.'

It was still snowing, large white flakes falling silently out of the sky above, and the wind, still as boisterous, was making them drift high against the hedgerows as Kate drove slowly up the hillside.

The gritters had done their job and the road was reasonable to drive along, until she turned onto the moors and found herself facing extreme blizzard conditions that almost made her miss the track that led down to Jane's cottage.

As she drove slowly along, with drifts on either side,

Kate was wishing that the old lady had taken the advice of others and moved to somewhere more accessible to avoid this kind of situation, but at least she'd managed to get to her. She would worry about getting back when she'd sorted Jane out.

The old lady managed to stay upright long enough to let her in by holding onto the furniture, and Kate saw immediately that she hadn't called her out for nothing. But she had known before she'd set off that Jane would never do that. She was a hardy old soul who didn't like to make a fuss.

After she'd examined her eyes and ears, felt her temples and checked her blood pressure, Kate informed her, 'Your blood pressure has taken a downward plunge and that is the reason for the dizziness. You are on medication for high blood pressure, aren't you? Sometimes it can bring it too low.

'Normally I'd put you on tablets to bring it back up, but tablets would take too long because of the severity of the dizziness. So I'm going to give you an injection, Jane, and then I think I need to take you to somewhere safer until the weather improves.'

'My sister lives in the village. I can stay there until the snow has gone,' Jane told her. 'She's always on at me to go and stay with her permanently. Maybe this is the nudge I've been needing. If anything happened to you because I'd called you out in this weather, I would never forgive myself.'

'Yes, well, let's not worry about that sort of thing just now,' Kate said after giving her the injection. 'Have you got a warm coat, boots and some blankets?'

It took some time to get Jane into her outdoor clothes

and wrapped in blankets in the front seat of the car, as she was still having difficulty keeping her balance. Once that was accomplished Kate went back inside to make sure that everything except the heating was switched off, and then turned her attention to the state of the weather.

It had worsened while she'd been sorting Jane out. The drifting snow was getting higher, the wind stronger, and she gave a sigh of relief when the car's engine started promptly.

But her troubles were not over. As she drove slowly up the incline that led away from Jane's cottage the tyres kept skidding on the snow and she was having difficulty seeing where she was going as the drifts on either side were closing in.

They were almost at the top when the wheels slid sideways and they became stuck in a deep drift, and no matter what she did the car wouldn't budge.

Jane was leaning back in the seat with her eyes closed as the injection was only just beginning to take effect, so Kate couldn't tell if it was registering when she said, 'We're stuck, I'm afraid, Jane, and will just have to sit it out until someone comes to find us.' I hope we don't freeze to death before they do, she thought, as it wouldn't be the first time someone had perished in a blizzard on the tops.

Daniel's house call had taken longer than he'd expected. He'd gone to visit the elderly father of the farmer's wife because he was generally unwell, and as he had pulled up outside the farmhouse the old man had suffered a heart attack and hadn't been breathing when he'd got to him.

It had been panic stations trying to resuscitate him and getting an ambulance to rush him to the nearest cardiac unit once he'd shown signs of recovery, and when at last he'd been able to check his messages on his mobile phone, he'd been horrified to hear from Jenny that Kate had gone to Jane Appleton's place and they'd heard nothing from her since.

A vision of Kate lying in the snow or having crashed the car in the icy conditions had come to mind. Don't let anything have happened to my beautiful girl, he'd prayed as he'd rung Jenny back.

'We've been trying to get through to her,' Jenny was telling him, 'but there's no answer.'

He nodded. 'Kate won't be able to get a signal out there. I'm going to go round to Jasmine Cottage to get blankets and a flask of something hot, and then I'm going up there, Jenny. You'll just have to cope the best you can without us, I'm afraid.'

'We'll cope all right,' she assured him, and he had disconnected and was getting into his car almost before she'd finished speaking.

When Ruth saw him pulling up outside she asked anxiously, 'Has Kate got back from Jane Appleton's, Daniel?'

He shook his head. 'Not yet. I've only just heard that she was called out by her and I'm anxious about her safety. I'm going up there to look for her, but first I'm going to phone the Mountain Rescue people to let them know they might be needed. While I'm doing that, could you find me some blankets and fill a flask with something hot?'

'Yes, of course,' she said, and hurried off to do as he'd asked.

When she came back he said, 'They've asked me to stay put and leave it to them, but I'm not hanging around here if Kate needs me. She could freeze to death if she's caught unprepared in this and the thought is beyond bearing.'

'Yes, indeed,' Ruth agreed, grim-faced. 'I didn't want her to go but she reminded me that she's a doctor and a patient was in need of her services.'

The last time Kate had checked her watch they'd been there four hours. Jane kept shivering and asking why they didn't go back to her house, and each time she had to explain that it was a good three miles back down the treacherous lane, and in any case they were stuck in the drift. Until someone dug them out or the snow began to thaw, they wouldn't be going anywhere.

Kate had taken off her top coat and wrapped it around her some time ago and now she too was battling with the cold, and as the minutes ticked by she was beginning to feel sleepy.

She'd been out of the car twice before it had become covered and had tried to dig them out with her shovel, but each time they were snowed in again within minutes, and now it was all around them, beneath and above. It was like being inside a cold white cocoon and every time she switched on the engine it just spluttered and died. The only good thing to happen since they'd left Jane's place had been the disappearance of the dizziness as the injection began to take effect.

Would she ever see Daniel again? she kept thinking. She didn't want to die without him having seen his ring on her finger.

The road to the moors was still open but the weather was worsening all the time and Daniel's anxiety was like a

giant beast gnawing away at him. He'd heard them talking
in the waiting room that morning about past tragedies out
there when motorists and walkers had underestimated the
ferocity of the elements. And if that old lady didn't move
to somewhere more sensible after exposing Kate to such
harm, he would want to know the reason why.

It was fortunate that he'd visited her before, he thought
as the turning that would take him to where she lived came
into sight in the swirling snow, and if by the time he
reached her cottage he discovered that Kate wasn't shel-
tering inside, the fear inside him would escalate.

As he eased the four-wheel-drive slowly down towards
the remote cottage there were high drifts on either side
and the only sound was the howling of the wind. Please,
let Kate be at the cottage, he begged the unseen fates, but
his plea wasn't answered. It was all locked up with no
signs of either doctor or patient, and with a sinking heart
he began the tortuous drive back up to the moors.

It was when he was almost at the top that he saw the
car stuck in a drift. Pulling up, he got out and slithered
round to the boot to get the shovel that Kate had warned
him he might need some time, never dreaming that it
would be for her he would have to use it one day.

He frantically shovelled the snow away from the scarlet
Mini that was dear to her heart, and wrenched open the door.

'You've never told me that you love me, Daniel,' Kate
said drowsily when she saw him.

'Not in so many words maybe, but I thought you'd got
the "drift",' he teased gently as he took her hand in his.

'The doctor would have me put *her* coat on top of mine,'
Jane said awkwardly, looking the perkier of the two.

'Well, yes, she would, Mrs Appleton,' he told her.

'Because that is what she's like. And now let's get you both into my warm car and take you to somewhere safe before we all get snowed in again.'

At that moment a helicopter appeared overhead and when it swooped down low, unable to land because of the rough terrain, the Mountain Rescue pilot shouted down, 'What's the score, Doc?'

'We seem to be all right. I'll know better when I get Dr Barrington and Mrs Appleton back to civilisation,' he bellowed back. 'But can you stay overhead while I'm driving back to the village in case we get stuck in the snow again?'

'Sure thing,' he said. 'I'll hover.'

He carried Kate limp and unresisting to his car, and as he wrapped her in a blanket he sent up a prayer of thankfulness. He'd found her safe and unharmed and joy bells were ringing.

When Jane was settled into the back seat he set off on the hazardous journey back to the village, thankful they were in a four-wheel-drive. Once he'd navigated the moors he found to his relief that the hill road had been gritted again and the snow had stopped drifting because the wind had slackened. On any other occasion he might have thought how enchanting everywhere looked, but not tonight.

He wanted to get Jane to her sister's and Kate back to Jasmine Cottage where her mother would be worried sick until he produced her daughter, very cold, wrapped in a blanket and sipping tea from the flask in a plastic cup.

After Kate had soaked in a warm bath and had some hot soup, she sat curled up beside the fire in the sitting room, dressed in a towelling robe. Grateful to be back in the warmth, and very much aware that every time she looked at Daniel he was smiling, but so was her mother, so was Tom. Only Alex was looking downcast.

He was seated beside her with the inevitable pencil and drawing paper and she said softly, 'Are you upset that we didn't get to make the snowman?'

'No,' he told her. 'Uncle Dan says we'll do it tomorrow. I thought that you were going to die too, Kate.'

She swallowed hard and wondered how she could bear to see him go when the time came for Tom to take him back to Gloucestershire. 'Come here,' she said, and when he got to his feet and came to stand in front of her, she reached out and held him close.

'I will always be there,' she told him. 'Wherever you are I won't be far away.'

'Do you promise?'

'Yes. I promise,'

'That's all right, then.' He went back to his drawing and now he was smiling, too.

It was almost midnight and all was still in the house when there was a knock on Kate's bedroom door. When she opened it Daniel was standing there, and as they faced each other he said in a low voice, 'Can I come in?'

She stepped back. 'Yes. I've been waiting until the others were asleep and then I was coming to find you.'

'I had the same thought,' he told her as he followed her into the room and shut the door behind him.

It was the first time they'd been alone since he'd found her in the snow and all evening she'd been remembering what she'd said when she'd seen him.

As she faced him, dressed in floral thermal pyjamas

that her mother had insisted she wear to ward off a chill after her ordeal in the snow, she said hurriedly, 'I hope you'll make allowances for what I said when you dug us out of the snowdrift. I wasn't quite myself at the time.'

He was laughing deep in his throat. 'I would say that you were exactly yourself. Uncomplicated, caring, completely adorable, and I am here to reassure you regarding the matter you mentioned.

'It might have been a long time coming but I'm here to tell you that I love you, Kate, more than I could ever have dreamed possible. I want you to be my wife, living in the house by the river with me and our children. The children that I'd always thought I would never have. Will you marry me?'

There was silence for a moment and then she held her hand out in front of her and the ring was there on her finger, the diamond dazzling as only diamonds do.

'I've been yours almost from the moment we met,' she said softly, 'but until now I've doubted that you would ever be mine.'

He had just made her feel beautiful and wanted in spite of the pyjamas and he was waiting for an answer.

'Yes, I will marry you,' she said slowly. 'Yes, I would love to live with you by the river. Yes, we will have babies and, Daniel, I will never begrudge you your memories of Lucy.'

'I know,' he said softly. 'Do you know how I know?'

She shook her head.

'I know because you are you. Kind and loving to all you meet. To me most of all. From the day we met, when I found you asleep in front of the heater, you have been gradually breaking down my defences. I thought I had my life mapped out, but I needed you to show me the way.'

'Just a few hours ago I wasn't sure whether I would ever see you again,' she said with tears threatening. 'But I should have known that a mere blizzard wouldn't deter you. Not only did you bring me home safely, you have just told me that we have a future together and I'm so happy, Daniel.'

'That's my girl,' he said tenderly as he took her in his arms. 'My beautiful, caring enchantress.' And when he'd finished kissing her until she was breathless he went on, 'Let's fix a date for the wedding.'

'I'd like to tell my mother first. She'll be overjoyed to hear our news, and mortified that she made me wear these pyjamas when the most wonderful moment of my life was about to happen.'

He smiled. 'You are beautiful to me no matter what you wear.' And just to make sure she had no doubts about that he took up where he'd left off.

Kate and Daniel told her mother their news before she came down to breakfast the next morning and, as Kate had prophesied, she was delighted, and not the least upset about the pyjamas.

'If the way Daniel looks at you is anything to go by, he won't be put off by a bit of thermal nightwear.' She chortled, and then on a more serious note said, 'From the moment you came to stay here, I felt I'd been blessed, Daniel, and now I know why.'

When they told Tom he smiled his satisfaction and, looking thoughtful said, 'Did I see an estate agent on the main street on the night you brought me here, Daniel?' And when he'd been assured that there was indeed such a place, he amazed them all by saying, 'Then maybe one of the staff could call round to show me what properties are on sale in the village. I'm retiring so there's nothing to stop us moving.

'Alex has already told me he wants to stay here, and from what I've seen of your village I can understand why. So we'll have to see what they can come up with.'

That brought smiles all round and Ruth offered immediately, 'You can stay here for as long as you like until you find something, Tom.'

'The house should be ready in the early spring,' Daniel told him. 'So I won't be taking up space here for much longer and Kate will be coming with me.'

'That's a very kind offer,' Tom told her, adding as Alex clapped his hands gleefully, 'I can see someone who will be loving that.'

'Didn't I tell you that I would always be near you?' Kate whispered in Alex's ear. 'Once the house is finished you can come and stay with us whenever you like.'

The following Saturday, the two doctors were enjoying a pleasant drive through the village. Every time Kate looked down at the ring on her finger it was like a dream, until she raised her head and met the dark hazel gaze of the man next to her, and then it became real. Blissful, wonderful reality.

They'd helped Alex to build the snowman that he'd waited so patiently for as soon as breakfast had finished, and now were driving to Jane Appleton's sister's in the next village, to check on the old lady after her ordeal of the previous day.

When they'd left her there the night before it had been

clear that her blood pressure problem had righted itself and she'd been well enough to walk into the house unaided. But they were both aware that they'd had to leave her rather abruptly and wanted to see for themselves how she was, *and* if it was convenient for her sister to accommodate her at such short notice.

They found her much steadier on her feet, so that was one worry off their minds, and Kate told her that as soon as she felt up to it she would like to see her at the surgery to have her medication for high blood pressure reassessed.

They were also relieved to hear that her sister was delighted to have her stay. She lived alone and it would be company for her.

'I've asked Jane to come and live with me many times,' she told them. 'But she always refuses.'

'Not this time,' Jane told her with a glance in Kate's direction. 'When I put someone in danger who has kindly come out to see me in vile weather, it is time to reconsider. I'll move here as soon as the snow is gone.'

As they drove back through the village to Jasmine Cottage, Kate glanced across at the window of the charity shop as they passed, and following her glance Daniel said, 'Any regrets that you didn't keep the wedding dress?'

'No. Of course not,' she told him. 'When I walk down the aisle to meet you my dress will be new and so beautiful it will make you go weak at the knees.'

He laughed and there was joy in the sound. 'The bride who will be wearing the dress has had that effect on me ever since we met, and nothing is going to change that.'

Daffodils were nodding their golden heads in cottage gardens and the green of the countryside around the village was deepening with the advent of spring on the bright April morning when Kate drove to the village church in an open carriage with Tom.

He was going to give her away. Slowly and laboriously he was going to take her down the aisle to meet her bridegroom. There would be gladness in his heart, and he knew that wherever she might be Lucy would not begrudge Daniel the love he had found with the radiant woman beside him.

In a dress of ivory brocade and carrying a bouquet of cream roses lovingly arranged by Sarah from the florist's, Kate was remembering that other wedding when she'd seen Sarah in the dress that had been hers and had known that she was free from it and all its associations.

It was because she'd met a man called Daniel Dreyfus, and today he was going to promise to love and cherish her for the rest of her life. The wedding dress that she was wearing today would not be going to the charity shop or back to the store. She would keep it for ever in the life that they were going to live together.

MILLS & BOON

Pure reading pleasure

APRIL 2008 HARDBACK TITLES

ROMANCE

The Sheikh's Blackmailed Mistress *Penny Jordan*	978 0 263 20270 0
The Millionaire's Inexperienced Love-Slave *Miranda Lee*	978 0 263 20271 7
Bought: The Greek's Innocent Virgin *Sarah Morgan*	978 0 263 20272 4
Bedded at the Billionaire's Convenience *Cathy Williams*	978 0 263 20273 1
The Billionaire Boss's Secretary Bride *Helen Brooks*	978 0 263 20274 8
The Giannakis Bride *Catherine Spencer*	978 0 263 20275 5
Desert King, Pregnant Mistress *Susan Stephens*	978 0 263 20276 2
Ruthless Boss, Hired Wife *Kate Hewitt*	978 0 263 20277 9
The Pregnancy Promise *Barbara McMahon*	978 0 263 20278 6
The Italian's Cinderella Bride *Lucy Gordon*	978 0 263 20279 3
Saying Yes to the Millionaire *Fiona Harper*	978 0 263 20280 9
Her Royal Wedding Wish *Cara Colter*	978 0 263 20281 6
SOS Marry Me! *Melissa McClone*	978 0 263 20282 3
Her Baby, His Proposal *Teresa Carpenter*	978 0 263 20283 0
Marrying the Runaway Bride *Jennifer Taylor*	978 0 263 20284 7
The Fatherhood Miracle *Margaret Barker*	978 0 263 20285 4

HISTORICAL

Untouched Mistress *Margaret McPhee*	978 0 263 20195 6
A Less Than Perfect Lady *Elizabeth Beacon*	978 0 263 20196 3
Viking Warrior, Unwilling Wife *Michelle Styles*	978 0 263 20197 0

MEDICAL™

Single Dad Seeks a Wife *Melanie Milburne*	978 0 263 19890 4
Her Four Year Baby Secret *Alison Roberts*	978 0 263 19891 1
Country Doctor, Spring Bride *Abigail Gordon*	978 0 263 19892 8
The Midwife's Baby *Fiona McArthur*	978 0 263 19893 5

MILLS & BOON®

Pure reading pleasure

0308 Gen Std LP

APRIL 2008 LARGE PRINT TITLES

ROMANCE

The Desert Sheikh's Captive Wife *Lynne Graham*	978 0 263 20034 8
His Christmas Bride *Helen Brooks*	978 0 263 20035 5
The Demetrios Bridal Bargain *Kim Lawrence*	978 0 263 20036 2
The Spanish Prince's Virgin Bride *Sandra Marton*	978 0 263 20037 9
The Millionaire Tycoon's English Rose *Lucy Gordon*	978 0 263 20038 6
Snowbound with Mr Right *Judy Christenberry*	978 0 263 20039 3
The Boss's Little Miracle *Barbara McMahon*	978 0 263 20040 9
His Christmas Angel *Michelle Douglas*	978 0 263 20041 6

HISTORICAL

Housemaid Heiress *Elizabeth Beacon*	978 0 263 20145 1
Marrying Captain Jack *Anne Herries*	978 0 263 20149 9
My Lord Footman *Claire Thornton*	978 0 263 20153 6

MEDICAL™

The Italian Count's Baby *Amy Andrews*	978 0 263 19944 4
The Nurse He's Been Waiting For *Meredith Webber*	978 0 263 19945 1
His Long-Awaited Bride *Jessica Matthews*	978 0 263 19946 8
A Woman To Belong To *Fiona Lowe*	978 0 263 19947 5
Wedding at Pelican Beach *Emily Forbes*	978 0 263 19948 2
Dr Campbell's Secret Son *Anne Fraser*	978 0 263 19949 9

0408 Gen Std HB

MILLS & BOON®
Pure reading pleasure

MAY 2008 HARDBACK TITLES

ROMANCE

Bought for Revenge, Bedded for Pleasure *Emma Darcy*	978 0 263 20286 1
Forbidden: The Billionaire's Virgin Princess *Lucy Monroe*	978 0 263 20287 8
The Greek Tycoon's Convenient Wife *Sharon Kendrick*	978 0 263 20288 5
The Marciano Love-Child *Melanie Milburne*	978 0 263 20289 2
The Millionaire's Rebellious Mistress *Catherine George*	978 0 263 20290 8
The Mediterranean Billionaire's Blackmail Bargain *Abby Green*	978 0 263 20291 5
Mistress Against Her Will *Lee Wilkinson*	978 0 263 20292 2
Her Ruthless Italian Boss *Christina Hollis*	978 0 263 20293 9
Parents in Training *Barbara McMahon*	978 0 263 20294 6
Newlyweds of Convenience *Jessica Hart*	978 0 263 20295 3
The Desert Prince's Proposal *Nicola Marsh*	978 0 263 20296 0
Adopted: Outback Baby *Barbara Hannay*	978 0 263 20297 7
Winning the Single Mum's Heart *Linda Goodnight*	978 0 263 20298 4
Boardroom Bride and Groom *Shirley Jump*	978 0 263 20299 1
Proposing to the Children's Doctor *Joanna Neil*	978 0 263 20300 4
Emergency: Wife Needed *Emily Forbes*	978 0 263 20301 1

HISTORICAL

The Virtuous Courtesan *Mary Brendan*	978 0 263 20198 7
The Homeless Heiress *Anne Herries*	978 0 263 20199 4
Rebel Lady, Convenient Wife *June Francis*	978 0 263 20200 7

MEDICAL™

Virgin Midwife, Playboy Doctor *Margaret McDonagh*	978 0 263 19894 2
The Rebel Doctor's Bride *Sarah Morgan*	978 0 263 19895 9
The Surgeon's Secret Baby Wish *Laura Iding*	978 0 263 19896 6
Italian Doctor, Full-time Father *Dianne Drake*	978 0 263 19897 3

MILLS & BOON®

Pure reading pleasure

0408 Gen Std LP

MAY 2008 LARGE PRINT TITLES

ROMANCE

The Italian Billionaire's Ruthless Revenge *Jacqueline Baird*	978 0 263 20042 3
Accidentally Pregnant, Conveniently Wed *Sharon Kendrick*	978 0 263 20043 0
The Sheikh's Chosen Queen *Jane Porter*	978 0 263 20044 7
The Frenchman's Marriage Demand *Chantelle Shaw*	978 0 263 20045 4
Her Hand in Marriage *Jessica Steele*	978 0 263 20046 1
The Sheikh's Unsuitable Bride *Liz Fielding*	978 0 263 20047 8
The Bridesmaid's Best Man *Barbara Hannay*	978 0 263 20048 5
A Mother in a Million *Melissa James*	978 0 263 20049 2

HISTORICAL

The Vanishing Viscountess *Diane Gaston*	978 0 263 20154 3
A Wicked Liaison *Christine Merrill*	978 0 263 20155 0
Virgin Slave, Barbarian King *Louise Allen*	978 0 263 20156 7

MEDICAL™

The Magic of Christmas *Sarah Morgan*	978 0 263 19950 5
Their Lost-and-Found Family *Marion Lennox*	978 0 263 19951 2
Christmas Bride-To-Be *Alison Roberts*	978 0 263 19952 9
His Christmas Proposal *Lucy Clark*	978 0 263 19953 6
Baby: Found at Christmas *Laura Iding*	978 0 263 19954 3
The Doctor's Pregnancy Bombshell *Janice Lynn*	978 0 263 19955 0